Mischief in Moonstone Series, Novella 3:
Mrs Claus and the Moonstone Murder

By Christine DeSmet

Writers Exchange E-Publishing
http://www.writers-exchange.com

Chapter 1

Lily Schuster was two days on the job as a county deputy serving Moonstone, Wisconsin, when she got a call about a trespasser-- digging for a giant beaver the size of a bear and scaring a lavender chicken.

Surely cleaning a nineteenth-century building in ninety-degree August heat had given her delusions.

She pulled her strawberry blonde hair off her perspiring neck and into a ponytail, then called her friend Kirsten Van Brocklin. They'd met in a Spanish class in Chicago a year ago.

Both women had been at crossroads in their lives, trying to leave dark shadows behind. Ironically, both had reasons to look to Moonstone, which sat on the shore of Lake Superior, for the answers they needed about their pasts. Kirsten's secret was exposed only a couple of months ago when she'd moved back to her roots in Moonstone to become a chef. In an almost unbelievable turn of events, Kirsten also became mayor--and last weekend,

Mrs. Jonathon Van Brocklin--after foiling the tycoon's topless fishing tour business.

Amid the wedding hubbub, Lily had read in the local newspaper about a special crime-fighting grant for rural northern Wisconsin. The feelings of revenge she constantly battled coursed through her veins again. Lily, who at thirty-four had no desire to return to the spotlight on the West Coast that had nearly destroyed her family, begged Kirsten to put in a good word for her. Lily got the job.

At Lily's mention of Tootsie Winters, who had called about the animals, Kirsten burst into laughter on the cell phone. "Watch out. This could be one of Tootsie's famous tests. When I was new, she pointed out all my so-called faults, such as my straight hair."

"Your hair was a problem?"

"Too straight, too white-blonde. That's Tootsie's way, pointing out the 'too's' in life. She and her husband Bob moved out of town last month to be closer to the docks over in Port Cliff where Bob runs his touring yacht. It used to be the topless fishing tour boat. He was mayor until the flap over the nude fishing gave him a heart attack. I'm betting Tootsie still wants the spotlight on her."

The mention of a spotlight sent sour panic into Lily's stomach. The one thing she needed most in life was to be taken seriously. Just once would be nice. "I'm supposed to be catching criminals, not chickens."

The cell phone practically vibrated from Kirsten's laughter. "Walk carefully around Toots...as if on egg shells--lavender egg shells!"

After goodbyes, Lily grimaced at the dirt on her yellow Green Bay Packer t-shirt and denim shorts. She dared not even brush at things. Who knew what microorganisms dwelled in a building constructed over a hundred years ago as a sundries store for lumberjacks. She moaned at her chipped manicure. A good manicure was a remnant from her past, but she didn't care. Even a woman deputy could be feminine. She needed to change clothes--and nail polish--so she looked professional for...a beaver-loving man and lavender chicken. And what was that about a nude fishing tour? *What has Kirsten gotten me into?*

Lily rushed about looking for her badge and handcuffs amid the junk she and Todd had brought up from the mouse-infested basement.

"Have you seen the handcuffs, Todd?"

Todd Arneson had walked in yesterday, a lanky, freckle-faced fourteen-year-old who was bored with summer. He had one week before school started. He was also six feet tall, so this morning she put a broom in the hands of "Tom Sawyer" and set him to wiping spider webs off the tin ceiling. With her grumpy boss coming for his first inspection next week, she was grateful for Todd's help, but he also proved mischievous.

He grinned down at her from the ladder. "Maybe your cuffs are in the basement."

Yesterday he'd gotten her twice with a cry of "Mouse!" She shuddered. "I'm not going down there again until we do something about the mice."

"I could bring ya some rat poison. Mom buys it in bulk for our motel."

Todd looked slap-happy as a naughty puppy. She admonished, "And I suppose you have a big fat rat for a pet. Now cough up the handcuffs."

He tossed them to her. "Is it really a giant beaver? Can I come along?"

"No." Lily used her handkerchief to swab a gob of spider web off the handcuffs. She put the hankie into a box with other rags to be washed, found her badge on top of the report she'd been reading about rural meth labs, then raced upstairs to her apartment to change.

Moments later, she headed out into the hot sun baking the sidewalk. She wore her brown uniform baseball cap, brown pants and short-sleeved shirt, with a fresh hankie tucked inside a pocket and her badge shined to match the sheen of her black shoes.

Todd scrambled after her. "Hey, you're bitchin'."

"Watch your language, kid." She hid a smile. It still thrilled her to see her reflection in the mirror, the cap brim just so over her eyes, hair out of sight, the yellow county logo with green pines on the sleeve.

She unlocked her side of the gray Honda Civic.

"Is the beaver alive?"

"He died some time ago," she said. "Now get back to work, please."

"Will there be maggots? If you have maggots you can tell how long somebody's been dead. I can help you figure out how long the beaver's been croaked."

Tow-headed Todd, who tugged playfully at the locked door, reminded her of her brother at that age, ready to embrace any adventure. Oh, how she missed that. Because of her brother she'd changed her life and career, starting over in her thirties. "Just this once you can go along."

Tootsie Winters, a stout, silver-haired woman wearing a matching top and shorts sporting red cherries, charged over as Lily got out of the car. The Winters' place, a few miles southeast of Moonstone, was a patch of sandy land carved from tall pine forest that abutted a marsh behind the peeling yellow house and weathered outbuildings. The humid marsh air feathered into the clearing carrying the scent of decaying leaves, pine needles, and...chicken crap.

Lily gaped at the ball of flyaway lavender fluff sitting contentedly in the crook of Tootsie's arm. Lavender fluff covered most of the chicken's unusual black legs. Even among all the fowl of San Francisco's Chinatown, Lily had never seen such chickens.

Todd laughed. "Looks like a hat."

Tootsie's scowl took the edge off Todd's fun. She pointed to a wire fence enclosure the size of a three-car garage. "See what he's done to my chicken yard? He's like a crazed rooster scratching about."

Several fluffy chickens of various colors--red, white, gray-blue, black-- moseyed about a man hip deep in a hole tossing dirt. The chickens with their strange legs looked like can-can dancers wearing black tights and fuzzy pantaloons. They appeared to vie for the man's attention. Lily could understand why. Her hand slipped inside a pocket to worry the hankie she always carried. She might need it to mop up her drool.

From this vantage point, he wore nothing but a bronze tan on well-defined back and shoulder muscles. The sun had lightened strands of wavy, chocolate brown hair that fluttered on his neck in the breeze. She understood the hens' urge to do-si-do up to him. She touched the badge on her pocket to quell her unprofessional reaction, but the dang shield vibrated from her ragged breathing.

Tootsie ranted on. "My prized chickens will fall in that hole. And why in heaven's name aren't you wearing a gun? My husband leaves me alone in the woods and this galoot needs to be warned. Where's your taser? Let's taser him. You look about as authoritative as my silkies."

Silkies? Was the woman talking about her underwear? Lily asked, "Who is he?"

"Marcus Linden. University big shot. He had a piece of paper he contends is a permit to dig here for beaver bones he says are ten thousand years old."

The lavender hen clucked at Todd. "She bite?" Todd asked.

"Heaven's no, not silkies. They love being petted, don't you, Lulu?" Tootsie said, stroking the chicken. "She's my prize. Lavender hues are the rarest. Had to drive down to Iowa for her." Tootsie handed the "hat" over to Todd.

Lily strode toward the chicken pen to meet the professor.

Once inside the gate, she picked her way around chicken poop landmines. "Hello?" She ducked to avoid flying dirt. She checked her shoes. So far, their polish remained pristine. "Mister Linden?"

Dirt smudged most of his body, though it didn't hide rippling biceps and forearms glistening with sweat.

Another shovel of dirt landed too close to be a mistake.

She leaped to the side, landing in chicken poop that spurted like gray toothpaste up the side of a black shoe. Her stomach twisted. "Do I need to arrest you?"

When he looked up, she was the one arrested by earthy brown eyes shaded with thick lashes. He cocked his head, challenging her with a sweeping smile that manacled her in place. "Arrest me. I'd be honored to spend some time with you."

She had a full view of a six-pack that led to low-riding denims. His gaze traveled up her form-fitting uniform, making the day hotter, making her grateful for chest pockets that covered up her body's surprising reaction. His large palms wrapped around the shovel handle, the fingers playing it, as if itching for another type of action.

Okay, he was an oaf, but she'd still be in college if her professors had looked like this guy.

She mentally slapped herself. He was acting like the same uber-smart, but smart-alecky, playboys hand-picked by her mother for Lily. She stepped back. Carefully.

"Get out of there," she ordered, looking down at him in the hole, her thumbs hooked at her pockets to keep her hands from shaking.

His demeanor shifted like the sun ducking behind a cloud. "I have a right to dig here, little lady."

He wasn't getting points for calling her "little". She tapped the badge on her shirt pocket. "Deputy Schuster. I'd like to see your permit and I.D., please."

"Pat me down." He raised his arms. "Deputy...Schuuuu...ster."

He said her name as if blowing her a kiss. Lily's throat went dry, but she had the urge to kick chicken poop at him for his insolence. "I need to see your permit."

He made a grand show of slipping his hands into all the pockets of his denim jeans, the jeans shifting low enough to make her swallow at the tiny stripe of soft-looking hair that trailed from below his belly button into the white band of his underwear.

"I forgot," he said. "Left everything in my cooler over there."

Oh great. She'd have to touch that red thing covered with dirt and chicken crap.

Inside the large, red soft-sided canvas cooler, she riffled through a messy microcosm of his life. She found a fat file labeled "Casteroides ohioensis", a calculator, bags of dirt samples and stone arrowheads, a cell phone, a GPS device, an old-fashioned compass, two salted nut rolls, a clear plastic container of...live, wiggling maggots.

She wrenched her hand back. Hearty laughter behind her made her grit her teeth.

"Need some help with my Maggie gals?"

She shuddered. *The man names maggots!* She retrieved a brown wallet from under the maggots.

His driver's license said he was six-two, twenty-nine, and mighty handsome with shorter cropped hair and the layer of dirt washed off. It was the best license photo she'd ever seen. His birth date made him a Taurus, a bull--bossy and stubborn. But she noted he was willing to donate his organs. That softened her toward him. But only a little. He'd be donating them sooner than he expected if he didn't cooperate. The thought renewed her sense of authority.

She took a folded blue paper from his wallet. "This permit is for the Wallenkamps' property, not Winters."

"The Wallencamps gave me permission. This was their land before they sold it to the Winters a month ago."

Now what? One glance back at the scowling Tootsie made Lily crouch down near the edge of the hole, her heart thundering. "Please, just come with me. Make it look good or that woman's going to cause us both huge headaches."

His firm lips wiggled inches from hers, making her swallow an unbidden itch to lean into what he was offering.

He swiped at sweat ebbing down his cheek, leaving a muddy streak. "No." He resumed digging.

Crap. Didn't her uniform mean a thing? The shiny badge? Even the red, black, and white fuzzy chickens wearing their pantaloons meandered up to peck at her uniform's brown fabric. When a white fluff ball settled between top of her shoes as if they were a nest, Lily grimaced.

Her nearly naked professor smirked. *How do you shake a sleeping hen off your shoes?* "I'll buy you lunch if you get this thing off me and come with me now."

"Deal. I'm starved." He climbed out of the pit to tower over her, holding out both wrists. "Handcuff me. Take me and have your way with me."

With the chicken nesting on her shoes, she couldn't move. Marcus Linden's aura smelled of salt, earth, and a sexiness that discombobulated her. All that was left for him to do was paw the earth like a Taurus bull. She stood like a frozen fool, a true rookie. Sweat poured down her spine, itching her back.

Fortunately, Todd yelled for her. "It's Kirsten on yer cell. She says some old fart's in bed with two women! And they're trying to kill each other. Come quick!"

Tootsie raced into the yard to pick up the white chicken. "Oh, honey, let me help you." She was talking to the hen, Lily noticed.

Marcus Linden winked. "Let's hold off on the handcuffs until later. You might need them for this next guy."

When the smug Mr. Linden turned back to his dig hole, Lily reacted by slapping handcuffs on him. It surprised even her.

"Hey!" he yelped.

"Hey, yourself. Get in the car."

Tootsie said, "Now that's more like it, Deputy."

Although Lily had control over Marcus, he smiled down at her with eyes shimmering. Lily's heart banged so hard against her ribs she was sure the badge was dancing. She stuffed him in the back seat of the Civic, along with a black t-shirt she'd spotted hung through a hole in the chicken wire fence.

From the shotgun seat in front, Todd asked Marcus, "Are you dangerous?"

"It seems I am to the female of any species."

"The Dep's okay. She hates mice. And getting her nails dirty."

"Todd!" Lily snapped at him, starting the car, spraying sand and red dirt behind them as she pressed the accelerator hard.

Marcus chuckled from the back. "You got Tootsie good. The white chicken, too. She looks pink now."

Lily died inside. She dared not even look in the mirrors. If any of this got back to her boss... She let Todd do the talking while she barreled down the road in the Honda.

Todd had twisted around in his seat belt. "You use maggots to clean bones?"

Marcus launched into a story about some zoo's buried hippo nearby that was being cleaned with maggots so the skeleton could be used in a zoology classroom. Lily could sense he was purposely trying to gross her out. She gritted her teeth, clinging to the steering wheel all the way into Moonstone, focusing on her chipped manicure.

Her nose wrinkled at the faint smell of chicken poop she'd forgotten to wipe off her shoes.

Chapter 2

The old fart was Henri LeBarron, eighty-four. He lived upstairs in the LeBarron mansion, known as the North Pole because of its green roof and red shutters, and because Henri had played Santa Claus for town celebrations for years until he'd become too frail, supposedly.

Kirsten, in white chef's hat and uniform, met Lily in the downstairs parlor with arms flailing at the staircase. "Ruth Mueller's up there in Henri's bedroom duking it out with some woman."

"Who's Ruth Mueller?"

"She used to play Mrs. Claus with Henri." Kirsten wrung her hands on her white apron. "You have to get them out of here. I'm trying to serve lunch."

The first floor dining hall in the back that overlooked Lake Superior had been converted to The Jingle Bell Inn, one of the area's finer restaurants. Lily bit her lip as she looked up the staircase, hearing screams. She didn't want to do it, but she rushed back outside to her car and unshackled Marcus. "I need your help splitting up this ménage-a-trois."

"Hold on. I don't have full professorship yet, no tenure yet. I'm an associate prof."

She tossed the black t-shirt at him. "Well, goody for you, Mr. Associate. Now associate with me. The last thing I need is to have my name in the paper, too. Move it."

She liked the taste of "move it" in her mouth. She especially liked that Marcus Linden followed her orders, though she was sure she'd glimpsed his mouth twitch toward a grin.

They hurried inside and up the stairs, following the sounds of a catfight.

A young, petite woman with a cap of glossy black hair and clad only in black lacy underwear held a gray-haired, spitfire of a lady in a headlock on the foot of the bed. The mattress squeaked and bounced. Henri, his mussed white hair rendering him more like Einstein than Santa, huddled against his pillows, the sheet drawn up over his bare chest. His eyes ping-ponged with the action.

Marcus rubbed his palms together. "I'll take the tough one." He grabbed for elderly Ruth, dressed in a torn red blouse and blue jeans.

Lily raced around the bed to pull at the gamine, who screamed, "Henri! Help me! Henri, I love you! I'm the one who loves you!"

Ruth flailed about like Fay Wray in the gorilla's arms. "Henri's mine! Has been since the eighth grade! I have the ring to prove it. I'm the real Mrs. Claus. Get your bony ass out of here!"

"My bony ass?" the imp spat back from across the bed. "Yours needs a good spanking!"

Lily wrestled the young woman toward a chair draped with clothing. "You, get dressed." To Henri, who was shivering under his sheet, she asked, "Mr. LeBarron, what's your story?"

But the younger woman spoke up. "We were having sex and this woman barged in."

Ruth growled from Marcus's clutches. "There was no barging. I've never had to knock before."

Henri blushed red as Ruth's blouse, but not from embarrassment, Lily noted, because his eyes looked like glittering disco balls. To Lily's dismay, Marcus winked at the old man.

Footsteps clattering in the hallway produced Kirsten and Tootsie, the latter breathing hard. "Another sex scandal in Moonstone?" *Puff.* "Wow." *Puff.* "We've gone from strippers in our past to nudie fishing, to a brothel now. Whaddya think, Mayor? A new slogan for Moonstone? Something like, 'In Moonstone, we moon you with a smile'."

Kirsten set her chef's hat straight. "I don't think so, Tootsie. Lily, please. I can't expect my customers to eat their apricot-stuffed trout and dandelion salads with it sounding like Miss Kitty's saloon."

Tootsie cooed, "Oh I just love 'Gunsmoke'. Thank God, for satellite dishes."

Lily held up her hands, thinking yet again what a mistake she'd made with this job. "If I have to, I'm going to arrest everybody right now."

"Arrest her," the young woman said, indicating Ruth before slipping into a white lace t-shirt and black jumper.

Henri and Marcus watched her dress with goofy grins on their faces. Lily wanted to leap across the bed to smack them both.

Lily helped the young woman zip up the back of her jumper. "Miss, tell me who you are for starters and there won't be any arrests."

"Felicity Starr, twenty-seven," the woman said, sniffling and applying lipstick the color of pink peonies to lips that blossomed all dewy on the spot. The males in the room sucked in a collective deep breath. "From East Peoria, Illinois."

"A trespasser," Ruth said, "and a gold-digger." She twisted in Marcus's hold.

"You and Henri know each other long?" Lily asked Felicity.

With pouty, movie star lips, Felicity smiled at Henri. "We met a week ago at the casino. We both like to polka."

Santa's cheeks glowed.

Ruth hissed, "See, she's after his money, not to mention his goodies."

Tootsie said, "I don't know, Ruth. All this because she likes to polka? That's not the same as pole dancing." She added for Lily's sake, "That's what Kirsten's grandma used to do."

Kirsten went red as a tomato under her white hat, but she was forming fists. Lily's friend liked to keep the past out of public discussions.

Before Lily could defend Kirsten, Ruth swatted at the air. "You heard Little Miss Muffet. She was at the casino! Her talents amount to lay one on me and let me lay you."

Marcus whistled. Lily was getting a headache. None of her training had gone over this morning's scenarios.

"I sew," Felicity huffed. "I made this jumper. I can make candles, bread, and pies."

"Pies?" Ruth said. "I just won the pie blue ribbon at the county fair. Henri, you can't possibly think her pies are better than mine."

Felicity smiled, batting her black eyelashes at Henri. "We haven't had time for dessert yet."

Still in Marcus's arms, Ruth spewed, "Try a knuckle sandwich for dessert."

Lily held out her arms again. "Stop. Both of you are leaving."

"We are not," the two women said in unison.

Crap again. Couldn't anybody do what she wanted them to do? *Just once?* "Okay. We'll..." What?

Tootsie piped up, "We'll have a bakeoff."

Kirsten's chef hat tipped sideways. "A bakeoff?"

"We'll make it a big event. Draw tourists in from the campgrounds to the downtown. The little trollop against the queen of pies. Henri finally gets his dessert when it's all over with--Ruth or Felicity."

Henri grinned, wickedly. "I like it. Whoever wins, I'll date you exclusively until my son Peter's wedding to Crystal Hagan come this Christmas. I'll choose the new Mrs. Claus as my date to their wedding."

Within moments, the old geezer had set up the contest. His manservant, Leonard Moline, a scowling Lincolnesque man with slicked-back, black hair and a dark suit, looked down his aquiline nose at everybody as he took notes. Each woman would make three types of pies of her choice, with the judging happening in the town square. Afterward the pies would be served at a party in The Jingle Bell Inn. Henri appointed himself and Tootsie--already preening--as judges, along with a friend of his, the famous reviewer from the Twin Cities' *Homestyle* magazine, Gigi Thorpe.

Kirsten twisted her apron. "Gigi? Reviewing my restaurant? I've heard she hates anything experimental and loves Chinese takeout, of all things. I'm ruined."

Lily's stomach gurgled. "I don't know, Kirstie, maybe you could cook Chinese while she's here. I've been missing Chinese food. There's nothing unless you drive an hour into Superior."

Marcus nodded, still holding Ruth. "You guys are also missing Mexican, Italian, African, Nepalese, and Russian."

Tootsie said, "Oh get a grip. We're not going to allow commie food in Moonstone."

It was Lily's turn to smirk at the confused Marcus.

Tootsie prattled on at Kirsten. "It's about time you expanded your menu beyond your garlic mashed potatoes. But you are serving those tonight, right? Bob and I are stopping by after I give the chickens a bath."

"I need a bath," the gamine said on a sigh.

Ruth said, "Let me help. I'll hold your head under water to make sure the space between your ears gets clean."

With wiggling eyebrows, Lily signaled Marcus to leave--with the women.

In the oppressive August heat outside, Lily got an uneasy feeling that this pie contest would end up with the proverbial pie or eggs on Lily's face--from lavender eggs of course. Tootsie chattered on about silkie chicken eggs being the best for the heart. She'd provide all the eggs for the pie meringue toppings and crusts.

Todd slid off the hood of Lily's Honda. "Hey, I know her." He pointed to Felicity getting into an older model, blue compact car. "She's staying at our motel. Shoulda seen all the suitcases, like she's gonna live here for good. Gotta go. See ya, Dep."

He raced across the street, then across the town square for Lily's building. He got into a car, presumably his mother's.

Marcus strode up beside Lily. Every hair follicle went on alert. The last thing she needed was his assessment of how she handled her second case.

He mused, "A pie contest to solve their love spat. Maybe you should deputize me for the big event, in case they end up tossing the pies at each other."

She knew him well enough already to expect a punch line.

He pulled up the front of his t-shirt to swipe at his forehead, giving her a view of a tanned six-pack that left her holding her breath. "I could really use a shower. Don't suppose I could use yours?"

"I don't have a shower yet," Lily said, grateful, because her imagination leaped ahead to a visual of her soaping his tanned chest, arms, the tanned legs and thighs, his tanned everything... "I just moved above that old store." She nodded in its direction. "The place has a chipped, claw-footed tub with iron stains I haven't been able to remove. And no shower, not even a hose."

"Maybe you should join me in the river. I'm out next to the Brule. Cool, clear water that moves fast around your body."

She had to admit that in this heat, with her uniform sticking to her back, it sounded inviting. "The river of Presidents," she muttered, trying to keep a bitter memory from tainting her words.

Eisenhower and other famous people--even Al Capone--had favored the area for its outstanding trout fishing and remoteness. Some said it was handy for burying bodies back then, too. The thought gave her pause. The area had robbed her family of somebody precious, too. She'd been hired because of criminal elements using the North Woods recently; everything was in place for avenging the past. "You're out there in a campground?"

"No. A canoe landing. Just me and the black bears and wolves."

Her insides leaned into protective worry. "I'll drop you off." She wanted to know where he was camping in case it was within one of the areas she'd been told to watch. A forester had been shot at last year in an area near the Brule. But there were miles and miles of the shallow trout river.

After dropping him off to retrieve his motorcycle parked at Tootsie's farm, she followed him south onto a desolate, red dirt fire lane. She rolled up her windows to keep out the clouds of red dust kicked up by Marcus's motorcycle.

They took several fire lanes, all miles long, carved in the thick woodlands. Thinking about her assignment, she looked for hunting shacks that showed signs of recent usage, or makeshift trails cut into the underbrush. She saw nothing. Relief puddled into her stomach for Marcus.

That relief was short-lived. After she pulled up to Marcus's modest, white RV, she turned the car around and was heading onto the dusty fire lane when she took one last look in her mirror. She almost ran into a tree. Marcus was obviously going for a swim in the cool, swift water of his beloved Brule River--naked.

Chapter 3

"Yes, everything was tan," a blushing Lily assured the curious Kirsten. Her friend had come across the square that evening after ten o'clock closing time at the restaurant. While Kirsten unpacked dishes and food staples in the white kitchen, Lily ironed white sheets she'd taken from the dryer down in the mouse-infested basement.

"Why didn't you join him?" Kirsten asked, fluttering her white-blonde eyelashes.

"I'm not here for a vacation. Or anything else." Lily pushed the iron along the sheet's decorative seam, her goal a smooth, perfect surface.

Kirsten hung new white mugs on hooks under the kitchen cabinets. "But maybe that's exactly what you need. Sex with no strings attached, sex with a professor, somebody not in the spotlight."

Lily looked up, iron in hand. "You did see the dirt on that guy? He's not coming anywhere near these sheets."

Kirsten laughed. "You're just not used to living with dirt. But deep down, isn't that why you leaped at the chance to come to Moonstone? To live a normal life?"

A tear bothered the corner of an eye. Lily pushed the iron across the sheet with vigor. "You're forgetting my brother. I have a job to do."

"You didn't come here for any old job. You came here because you feel an obligation to your brother. Lil, don't let that obligation possess you."

Lily shrugged off the arrow that had hit its target. She moved the sheet forward on the board.

Kirsten clanked earthenware plates into place in a cupboard. "How's your brother doing?"

Lily shook with the anger that always erupted when she thought about Jason. "He skipped out on rehab."

"Oh, no, I'm sorry."

Lily zapped away the rumples in the sheet, ironing out the imperfections, feeling the rush of it, wishing she could do the same for Jason. "I traced Jase's credit card purchases. He bought a plane ticket for Santiago, Chile, of all places. He's on the run, getting as far away from his family as he can go."

When Kirsten gave her a hug, Lily's anger slunk back into its cave. They folded the sheet together.

Kirsten said, "This pie bakeoff between the floozy and the foolish Ruth is just the kind of fluff you need in your life. That and your naked man digging for a beaver out there on the farm with the lavender chicken. You realize, of course, that he's exactly the earthy type of guy that your mother and dad would hate to see you marry."

Lily gave in to a hearty laugh, pulling a brown uniform shirt onto the ironing board. "Don't try using my parents' wishes to throw me together with some professor who loves grubbing around in dirt and chicken crap. We're opposites."

"How so? Besides the dirt thing? You know, it might be fun to wash him off yourself sometime."

Lily's hands trembled. She had the iron poised above the pockets of her shirt. She recalled the way she'd tensed in a womanly way when he'd stared at her that morning. "For one thing, the man has no respect for my uniform."

Kirsten guffawed, her blonde bob swishing about. "You mean he likes no clothes and you like too many."

"That's not fair. My job calls for proper attire."

Kirsten busted open another cardboard box. "Those are short-sleeved shirts you're ironing. You're ironing a crease in about four inches of cloth. They don't need ironing. And the pants. Look at those creases." She pointed at the hangers lined up on the kitchen window curtain rod.

Lily frowned. "What's wrong with them? Should I re-iron them?"

Kirsten laughed. "They're wash-and-wear uniform pants. You don't need to iron them. You're obsessed with being in uniform. And with ironing."

"I like to iron. It's soothing."

"Don't you dare try to tell me ironing is like a mini-vacation. And don't fault your beaver man for being a free spirit. You used to be one. How you could've given away all those expensive skirts and tops your mother bought... I hope this man's habits rub off on you a little. Better yet, I hope he rubs up against you and irons your personality wrinkles out!"

"Kirsten!"

Kirsten continued to test Lily over the next three days, through Friday of that Labor Day weekend, the day before the pie bakeoff. Kirsten insisted that Marcus had the big-city palate she needed to try out new recipes that Gigi Thorpe might like. So she sent Lily out to the chicken farm with lunch each day for her prime taste-tester, Marcus. Knowing Kirsten was matchmaking, Lily complained that she hadn't been able to watch her noon-hour soap opera for days.

"I'm recording it for you," Kirsten said, handing her a sandwich layered with a garlic mashed potato pancake, a perch fillet, and coleslaw.

Lily sniffed the garlic hanging in the humid air. "When are you going to create Chinese for me? All of these recipes seem to be for Marcus. Should I be telling your husband about this?"

Kirsten pushed her out the door. Lily added, going to her car, "I get no respect for this uniform. Do I look like a delivery service?"

"Well, you are wearing brown."

The trips to see Marcus became the mini-vacations Kirsten had suggested Lily needed, though she'd never admit that to her friend. Watching his muscles ripple while he shoveled, watching him kid around with the silkie hens, watching him get an orgasmic look on his face when eating--intrigued Lily. The man enjoyed everything full-tilt while she held back, hidden behind her uniform. But he gave her dreams in the night that rousted her to turn the air conditioner on high, splash her face with cold water, and strip out of her nightshirt while wondering exactly how cold was the Brule River?

She justified the farm trips by using them to explore the little-used back roads where meth labs could be set up. Unfortunately, Todd had found her meth lab reports and maps. Earlier that Friday, just before she'd left to pick up the fancy sandwich for Marcus, he'd said, "Caught another mouse. Wanna see it?"

"No."

"His head was squished by the trap. Knocked his brains out. Found one at home like that with maggots in it, too."

"Todd, please, get back to work. And no more maggots, okay?" He was man-handling a buffing machine on the oak plank floor. He'd stripped the wood the day before of its brown paint, revealing a golden sheen today.

"You need something like that to catch those drug dealers."

She stopped on her way out the front door. "What're you talking about?"

"A big mouse trap. For what they did to your brother."

She froze. "How do you know about my brother?"

The kid leaned over the buffer handle. "The picture's in the file about the meth labs."

"Did you read all my reports?"

He flashed a sheepish frown. "Naw. Most of the paragraphs were too long."

She could breathe again. "You stay out of my files from now on or you can't work here. Deal?"

"Okay. Sorry."

She gave him a grin. He was only a kid. She should've locked up her reports. "I'll bring you back homemade black raspberry ice cream from The Jingle Bell Inn later."

Todd gave her a thumbs up.

Watching Marcus and the colorful silkies watching him, too, gave her a good diversion from thinking about meth labs, her brother, and dead mice. The chickens piled practically on top of each other to snooze like girls on one bed at a slumber party. Lily had never had a slumber party; she'd never had close friends when she was little because her mother kept her busy with acting lessons and similar irritating activities. Watching the hens sharing their girlie secrets sent an odd tug to Lily's heart. She couldn't figure out the feeling.

Marcus exacerbated the feeling with his exuberance about the silkies. "They're missing their barbules, the shaft in the feathers. That's why they're hairy."

"Oh." *Thanks, Professor.* Lily leaned on her car hood outside the pen every day, never having an answer for his insatiable appetite for new facts about every little thing.

"Lulu's the only one having sex with the rooster."

"Oh." Lily had yet to see the rooster, who stayed inside mostly. If he looked anything like this professor, she'd say, *You go, Lulu!*

Lily always ended up pacing to quell the silliness of her thoughts. They were decidedly "un-uniform" thoughts.

Marcus worked nonstop every day, driven to find his beaver, which Lily understood would help him garner that tenure he desired. It struck her that she and the professor had one thing in common--their drive to be respected in their profession.

Lily also admired her recipe-testing professor for the deal he brokered with Tootsie that Friday.

"I'm throwing new shingles on that chicken coop and painting it after I find my beaver bones."

"Don't you have to go back and teach in Madison?"

"Oh yeah, but I figure it's the least I can do to keep her off your back about all this digging. I'll drive up weekends to get it done for her before the snow flies."

"That's nice of you." *Nice for me.* He'd already become her habit. Now the idea of him staying on spawned a feeling inside that almost made her want to cluck, too. A warmth spread through her limbs at the prospect of...*seeing him with a lumberjack's flannel shirt on against the autumn chill, my head snuggling into its softness as we share a walk arm-in-arm through the woods, the heart-shaped golden birch leaves strewn in front of us as if the forest path is our bridal aisle.*

Good grief but she'd been listening to Kirsten too long. Lily went to the chicken wire gate to retrieve Marcus's proffered luncheon foam clamshell.

"How was it?"

"Wonderful!" He winked at Lily. "Maybe you could convince her to make one of those sloppy Italian meatball sandwiches."

"Kirsten won't even consent to Chinese egg rolls, even though Gigi likes them. She insists Gigi's going to be impressed with her new twists on sandwiches and omelets, the staples of life."

Tootsie came their way. "I need to get the eggs for the prospective brides for all those pie meringues and custard sauces."

Marcus opened the gate for Tootsie. "I'll help. I cleaned around the coop." To Lily he said, "Probably safe for you to come in, too, Deputy. No need to take the shoes off or anything."

Lily grimaced at the joke. The tall, muscular man took his time moving the delicate fluffy hens while Tootsie gathered eggs. When he petted lavender Lulu, Lily experienced an odd pang of jealousy. That was when she saw the beguilement on Tootsie's face.

When Tootsie left for town with the eggs, Lily said, "Have you noticed how she fusses about out here, panting, and not from the heat?"

Marcus looked down at Lulu in his arms. "Lulu? Oh yeah, she's my gal."

Lily bit the inside of her cheek to keep from mentioning Tootsie.

Marcus scratched Lulu under her hairy chin. The hen's eyes closed in an ecstasy that made Lily shift in her stance. Marcus said, "You seem to be the only one I can't charm."

"I'm on duty."

"When are you off-duty? Tonight? I've got a bottle of wine chilling in the Brule. You can watch me make my notes for my book about the giant beaver. I'd love your opinion. I don't want it to be too academic." He kept petting Lulu. "It's a children's book. Maybe someday your kids will read it in school."

"I haven't thought that far ahead in life."

"I assumed that's why you ended up here in this beautiful area. To raise a family." He breathed in deeply. "Smell that air."

"I smell chicken poop."

"It's good fertilizer. You can bring your kids out here to see Lulu and her progeny in years to come, collect shovels of chicken poop for your garden, and tell your kids about the writer you handcuffed once upon a time."

The breeze bent the sunlight coming through the leaves of the birch trees and branches of the pines. She could smell her future, sweet, yet pungent with mystery. Kids? If she had a girl, she'd get a slumber party. Marcus's nigglings made her yearn to iron something just to ponder it all. Her mother would never like him. That reality smacked Lily. She couldn't fall for a guy because her mother would hate him, no matter how inviting the thought.

She passed on his offer. It helped that she was busy that Friday night and Saturday morning preparing the town square for the pie bakeoff. The streets became clogged; Lily stood at intersections to signal cars toward the school's playground to park.

Kirsten had spent town money on clowns, face painters for the kids, and a small polka band. Card tables with homemade goods, including Kirsten's mother's decorated birdhouses, dotted the area sidewalks.

All was well, Lily noted, until the bakeoff, when the hoity-toity grand dame of food reviews, Gigi Thorpe, took her third bite of banana cream pie with meringue frosting, then fell dead.

Lily called an ambulance.

Standing next to the picnic tables with the pies, Ruth pointed at Felicity. "You poisoned her."

"How can you think that?"

"Clean your ears, honey. It was your pie."

The crowd surged in to look at the fifty-five-year-old woman on the ground in the tailored aqua suit with a hunk of banana cream sliding from the corner of her lips.

Lily pushed people back. "Folks, nobody poisoned anybody."

Volunteer EMTs showed up within only a couple of minutes, but they pronounced Gigi dead at the scene. The word "murder" became a buzz as irritating as a deer fly aiming to chomp on Lily's head.

Marcus rushed up to her, whispering, "I overhead somebody on their cell talking with Gigi's newspaper. It could be only a matter of an hour or so before a helicopter drops a TV news crew here from the Twin Cities."

He'd taken a shower somewhere. Tootsie's place? He smelled like lemony soap, had his hair combed back except for the unruly waves gracing his forehead, and wore khaki shorts and a white polo shirt. She wanted him to whisk her away from all this nonsense.

"At least I did my nails last night," she said, offering him a bleak grin. "Bring on my photo op."

"You don't mean that."

"Of course not. Let me think."

Lily appreciated his stance between her and the crowd. It gave her a moment to make a decision in private.

She went to get her evidence collection kit from the trunk of her car, though she couldn't quite figure out what to do except to put on the gloves and bag all the pies on the table. She knew if she didn't do everything possible--make it look good in case this was murder--that she'd be in the news instead of Gigi.

Marcus helped keep the crowd away from the evidence on the picnic tables: banana cream, lemon meringue, rhubarb crunch, apple, blueberry, and chocolate pudding pies.

Ruth stepped forward. "Henri could've died. He was next in line to taste the pies."

Seated in his wheelchair nearby under the big oak tree, Henri sweated profusely. "Maybe you wanted to make me sick, Ruth. Maybe you hoped to warn me off Felicity. Maybe you killed Gigi instead."

Ruth fainted. Her head barely missed the corner of the picnic table.

Several people eased her to the ground. Marcus hurried off to a lemonade booth and came back with a cold drink to help revive her.

The crowd stared at Lily like curious cows in a field waiting for excitement. Lily's armpits pumped out sweat but her brain wasn't telling her what to do next.

As usual, Tootsie helped things along. With Lulu in her arms, she said, "So that's how you command the situation? Standing around?"

Being shamed by a lavender chicken worked.

"Everybody," Lily commanded, "stay where you are." She climbed on top of the picnic table, careful not to step on the pies. "Mister Linden is coming around with a piece of paper. I need all your names. As soon as you give me your home address and phone number, you can go."

Murmured objections sent a shiver down her arms. She adjusted her ball cap, hoping she could acquire a sinister look. "I'm sorry, but I must insist or I'll...have to haul in those who object."

That sounded good.

A man in a fishing hat raised his hand. "Where's the jail here in Moonstone?"

Telling them it was a mouse-infested basement wouldn't sound good. She planted her feet apart and scowled, affecting a deep voice. "You don't want to know."

The man flinched.

Marcus gave her a secretive thumbs up. She handed him Gigi's notepad and pen left behind on the table. Marcus thrust them at Leonard Moline first. He took a huffy breath, but signed the paper. Lily was sure Leonard was trying to contain a smile, oddly enough. He pushed Henri's wheelchair toward the North Pole mansion across the street. Felicity rushed over, but Leonard rebuffed her. Lily found it curious that Henri didn't come to Felicity's defense. Felicity slapped at tears as she rushed to her compact car.

Lily watched the crowd signing the notepad, making a mental list of who might have had access to the pies and reason to poison somebody. Kirsten rushed off mumbling that she needed to make dessert at The Jingle Bell Inn because the pies weren't on the menu anymore. Lily flinched at the thought of Kirsten being involved, but she had to put her on the list because Ruth had used her restaurant kitchen to bake her pies.

Tootsie had brought the eggs to both women, so she was on the list. Did the former mayor's wife want the spotlight back on herself and Moonstone, even if it was via bad publicity?

Ruth got up from the lawn, scrambling to get on her bicycle to pedal away, maybe too fast--to avoid speaking with Lily? Maybe Ruth wanted Felicity blamed for the murder and had planted poison in Felicity's pie somehow?

What about Henri? Besides Tootsie, he was the only other one behind this pie contest. Did he use it to try to get rid of Ruth or Felicity so he could finally be at peace in bed with the woman of his dreams? But who was that? Was he merely using Felicity to tease Ruth, his desired Mrs. Claus?

She took out her cell phone and called the sheriff, who recommended she call in the Department of Criminal Investigations (DCI) because the case involved a famous person. She didn't mind the help. She hoped DCI and the coroner could determine overnight that Gigi wasn't poisoned, so that Moonstone could settle back to normal. Lily wanted to get back to the matter of payback for her brother.

Marcus handed her the notepad swimming with signatures and addresses. "You don't look so good."

"It feels weird hoping Gigi only died of a heart attack."

He settled three bagged pies on each long, bronzed forearm. "Where to?"

He made her smile. "You were a waiter in your past?"

"For years at a lovely Italian restaurant on campus, until I got my Ph.D. in paleontology. Where do you want them?"

"For now, I guess in my refrigerator. Until the DCI guy gets here."

"I'll wait with you."

Her heartbeat flip-flopped. She didn't want him sensing how scared she was about her first real crime case. Saving a lavender chicken from trespassing bone collectors was starting to sound preferable. "That's not necessary."

"I'm your witness. Nobody can accuse you of tampering with evidence. Just tampering with me."

Despite being weary, her body hummed at his flirtation. But there was more to it than mere flirting. She needed an ally, a friend. Being the sole law officer in a small town was lonely. Having to prove herself every minute got tiring, too. She accepted his help.

Marcus put the pies in her refrigerator.

She also enjoyed the way his tan, dark hair and chocolate-colored eyes stood out in her white kitchen. It was as if her apartment made him more alive. "Would you like a soft drink? Chocolate milk?"

"I need a good strong drink. Chocolate milk on the rocks."

"You got it."

While she poured the milk, he went to the ironing board where she'd left a stack of ironed, folded white pillowcases. *He lifted one up to smell it!* She almost poured milk on the floor. What was he doing being intimate with her pillowcases?

She brought him the iced milk.

Finally he put down the pillowcase. "Sorry. It's just that it's been a whole summer since I've slept in a good bed with great smelling sheets. My mom always puts hers out on the line. We have lilacs. In May, when she brings in the sheets they smell like lilacs."

She wondered what he thought her sheets smelled like. When he didn't fill in the blank for her, she said, "I iron my sheets. That's all it is. Clean sheets warmed up."

"Happy sheets. I guess I need a good woman to come out and make my sheets happy."

A tickle erupted in a place she couldn't scratch. "How long has it been since you washed any of the sheets in that motor home?"

When he had to think about it, she found that endearing. Maybe he did need a woman like her.

From maggots to lilacs, he was more complicated than she first thought. But she couldn't let herself get involved with Marcus Linden. This was short-term stuff no matter which way she looked at it. He'd dig up his beaver bones, after he painted Tootsie's coop, and be gone by Halloween. He'd get his tenure, publish his children's book, then dig up more bones. He'd become famous, give speeches at conferences, be invited to museum fundraisers. Lily's mother would love him.

She smiled across the table at him after he sat down. "My mother spends tons of money on laundry services that infuse her sheets with all kinds of chemicals. I like your mother's methods better."

He took a swig of chocolate milk. "Doesn't always work. One time the neighbors next door evidently had a big cook-out while we were gone. The sheets smelled like barbecued brats and burgers."

"She had to re-wash them?"

"Heck no. She's too practical for that. I went to bed every night for a week salivating onto my pillowcase, dreaming I was eating giant brats and burgers."

She laughed. As he launched into other silly family stories, she let herself ease into his rhythms. He talked with wild gestures that made her think of him as a symphony conductor, drawing her in, making her lean one way then another with the timbre of his voice. Fortunately, the DCI guy from Superior came within the hour.

Lily watched Marcus leave on his motorcycle, finally watching nothing but the air and listening to his engine until it evaporated, too.

She ran cool water in the rust-stained tub. Instead of relaxing her, though, the tub with its still water seemed to suffocate.

She got out, wrapping a towel around her. She wandered to the kitchen to finish off the cold milk, but as she opened the refrigerator door, the stack of pillowcases drew her to the ironing board. She touched the folded pillowcase, laying her fingers over Marcus's indentations.

Lifting the pillowcase, she smelled it. He'd called them happy sheets. But what had he smelled? He'd never told her. She sniffed the white percale again. She smelled ordinary mild detergent in pedestrian two hundred fifty count material. Her mother would be appalled. Lily smiled.

She understood why she hadn't been comfortable in her tub of still water. She longed for a swim in the chilly currents of the free-flowing Brule River. But did she want to be with Marcus because her mother and father wouldn't approve of him? For all his life he could earn a modest professor's salary, maybe publish his one children's book about a giant beaver, and that'd be the extent of his fame and fortune.

Falling for a guy when on the rebound from your parents' meddling wasn't right or fair, Lily concluded. It was best to leave him to charm Lulu the lavender chicken and Tootsie Winters.

Chapter 4

Kirsten called Lily on Sunday morning a little past ten in a panic. Locals, campers, and other tourists had packed The Jingle Bell Inn to eat scrambled eggs with a side of gossip.

Kirsten pleaded, "Can you go out to Tootsie's for more eggs? Stop by here first and I'll send you out with an omelet for your beaver man."

"He's not 'my' beaver man. He's all wrong for me."

"How so?"

That made an omelet of her brain. "He's five years younger than I am. I checked his license."

"Aha!"

"I'm only stating the facts." Lily sat down with the phone at her kitchen table, sipping black coffee while staring at a copy of the Minneapolis paper. She'd driven all the way into Superior for a copy. Gigi Thorpe's unnaturally smooth face stared back at her. "Five years is a lot. I'm on my second life already, and he's still on his first one."

"So your eggs are getting old. All the more reason to take him up on his offers."

Lily frowned into her cup of black joe. "Did you put him up to asking me out?"

"He did?"

"I bet you even bought my favorite wine and gave it to him to cool in the river."

"How romantic."

The newspaper headline read, "Food critic takes last bite". Lily found that a bit ingenuous. She sighed into the phone. "You got me this job and now you want to fix me up with a family? When did you talk with Marcus?"

"I passed your prisoner notes about you in the lunches I sent out with you."

"That definitely feels illegal. I *am* the deputy sheriff."

"Yeah, and I bet you're even sitting there in full uniform at your kitchen table on a Sunday morning."

"So?"

"You should be dressed in nothing having coffee in Marcus's RV. You told me in Chicago you wanted nothing more than the small town life where you could raise kids right, not like you and I were raised, me in the strip club and you doing kiddy beauty pageants. Why don't you go out and get dirt under your nails? Why not dig up bones with Marcus?"

"Now you want me to get friendly with dirt? I hate dirt! I've never lived with dirt. I don't know what it's made of but it can't be good."

"There are scientific formulas for dirt. Wisconsin has even named a state soil. If you're going to live here you need to learn this stuff. You must embrace dirt."

Lily glanced at her perfect fingernails. "I feel like I'm in church being preached at."

"That's another thing. You missed church this morning. Why?"

Lily smiled. She'd lingered in bed, her head resting on the pillowcase Marcus had touched. That was going to have to be her secret, though. She took a big slurp of coffee, letting it burn her throat. "DCI called this morning. Gigi Thorpe was poisoned. The coroner and DCI are working on identifying all the poisons."

"Oh my gosh, do you know what this means?"

"Gigi's dead?"

"No. Reporters have to eat. They'll go home and spread the news about my restaurant."

"Aren't you even a little bit sorry she's dead? You're sounding like a suspect."

A loud click at her window drew her across the apartment to look down on the street. Todd smiled up at her with one arm raised back with a piece of gravel between his fingers. "Hey, Dep, what ya need me to do today?"

She welcomed the teenager's diversion. Kirsten's mention of reporters swarming Moonstone sat in Lily's stomach like bacon grease. She went downstairs to give her Tom Sawyer his job for the day.

Lily had to stop this nonsense of seeing her beaver man every day. She was about to be descended on by journalists, who might dig up her own past in kiddy beauty pageants. *Live that down when you're trying to solve a murder.*

She thought about digging in the omelet she brought Marcus late that morning to check for another note. But what she needed more than lovers' notes were quick answers to the case of Gigi Thorpe's death.

Shirtless, sweaty, and sexy as hell, Marcus didn't help her resolution to maintain professionalism. She stayed outside the chicken wire enclosure, convincing herself that he was too much of a big smudge of dirt for her to handle. The woman married to him would need a good hose at the back door and a high-end washing machine.

He stopped tossing dirt when Lily told him about the findings. "More than one poison?"

"They think they've got household chemicals in the pie. She likely reacted to them fast, an allergic reaction. It'll take them a couple of days to be sure what all was in the pie."

"Need my help?"

She held up The Jingle Bell Inn bag. "I came out to get eggs for Kirsten. And to give you lunch."

"Better not be pie."

She grinned, grateful for his tease. "An omelet. One of Kirsten's new recipes Gigi was supposed to sample had she lived. Instead of vegetables, it's filled with flower blossoms and goat cheese from a friend's goats."

"Do I look like a guy who eats flowers?"

"I'm pretty sure you ate dandelions the other day without even knowing it. She used them in the coleslaw that was on that perch sandwich."

He waved her off. "You haven't eaten since before the pie contest, have you?"

She shook her head.

"Eat the omelet. Tootsie made me pancakes with homemade blueberry syrup, sausages, and Priscilla's eggs."

"Priscilla?"

"The blue chicken." He nodded toward the coop where the fluffy hens sat contentedly outside, under a bench on nests made of straw. "The red ones--the color's called partridge, Tootsie says--are Ruby and Raspberry. The white silkie's Wilhomena. The buff is Beulah, the black hen's Harriet, and the black rooster courting Lulu is Sydney Poitier."

Again, Lily struggled with the strangeness of jealousy.

She pulled her ball cap further over her eyes. "Is Tootsie here? I'd like her advice." And the low-down on why she was entertaining Marcus.

"She and Bob needed to clean their yacht before a party cruise in the afternoon. Loaded up their car with stuff."

"Cleaning supplies?"

"You think she may have taken supplies to make sure you didn't find them here? You can't think Tootsie murdered Gigi?"

"I don't trust Tootsie."

He climbed out of the hole, unfolded a three-legged camp stool, and sat down on the other side of the fence like a priest listening to Lily's confession. "You're thinking Tootsie wanted all this to happen?"

"The bakeoff was her idea. She loves to make things happen in Moonstone. You should see the town. All the shops are booming." *Not to mention my cell phone with its twenty messages from journalists already.*

"But she loves her chickens. I can't see her betraying them."

"You talk like they're persons."

He shrugged. "Each has her own personality. They're the best mothers, too."

"Mothers?"

He thumbed toward Lulu snuggled into the last nest under the bench. "Lulu finally laid an egg. Won't hardly leave the nest. But when she does, one of the other gals moves right in. I take breaks to go over and scratch their necks. That seems to relieve their anxiety over caring for the new clutch. Course, Tootsie says this could go on for a few days, until maybe even a dozen little Lulus are laid."

Lily stared gape-mouthed at him, her brain stalled on the vision of him soothing her when Baby Number One, Two, and Three, heck, a whole clutch came along. Her mother would hate having a daughter who had become a "mere" mother to a brood, which made Marcus all the more attractive at the moment.

Lily backed away from the fence and Marcus. "I need to get back to town."

"I better gather the eggs for you. Not Lulu's of course."

He petted each colorful, fluffy chicken. When they clucked, he clucked back. His intonations varied by chicken as he gathered the eggs. *He's having a conversation with chickens! Why doesn't he coo at me like that? Why do I get the jokes instead of the cuddly stuff?*

Beaming, he came through the gate to present a basket full of brown eggs. "Anything else for milady?"

Yeah, scratch my neck, too, scratch everything! The overwhelming need for him scared her. She appreciated that her uniform stopped either of them from doing anything stupid. "I better hurry or Kirsten will scramble me instead of these eggs."

She was opening her car door when her dread of facing the murder case alone smacked her again like an ice cream headache. She'd become used to being with this man over a mere five days, going on six. What harm could come with admitting they were friends? He was leaving this coming week, after all.

Marcus had already returned to his dig hole.

She hurried back to the fence. "Marcus, there's a way you can help me solve this case fast. Would you...be my partner of sorts?"

"I'm busy, getting close to the strata where I could find my *Castoroides* boy."

"Castor boy isn't going anywhere. My clues might dry up if I don't pursue them now." What was it about this man that he would have breakfast with Tootsie and her chickens and not want to come along with Lily? There had to be something wrong with herself besides the uniform, but what?

He wandered over to hang one index finger on a hole in the fence in front of her face. "What exactly do you want me to do?"

Her mind saw happy sheets. Her badge rattled over her foolish heart. "Look sexy."

"Whoa. This is a joke, right?"

"Women use their bodies all the time to get what they want from men."

"You're experienced?"

Did he have to frown like that? "None of your business. And this is business. I want to use your body and charm to loosen women's tongues. A drooling woman confesses to all sorts of things she wouldn't otherwise."

A grin spread across his face. The brown eyes glinted. Lily expected him to crow like Sydney the rooster. He tapped the end of her nose with the index finger poking through the fence. "Strictly business?"

"Of course."

"I don't know. I wouldn't want people thinking I was your boyfriend. That could destroy your image, your ability to work. I better pass."

Double crap. So much for happy sheets with him. She'd try another tack, anything to make herself attractive somehow. She couldn't lose to a bunch of hens. "Marcus, you can be my boyfriend." His eyelids popped wide, which made her all the more confused. "Because I've got lots of boyfriends back in San Francisco. You wouldn't be anything special."

She died inside. That hadn't come out right. But her mother indeed had an entire list of guys at the ready with marriage proposals. "So you'll come with me and help?"

Marcus blinked several times, wincing, as if she'd gotten in his eye and he wanted to dispose of her. "Hell, no. You don't need me."

Embarrassment burned her forehead. "Fine, then, I'll get on with my job."

After delivering the eggs to The Jingle Bell Inn, a bereft Lily drove to Ruth's house. Steel puffs of clouds moved in from the lake, elbowing out the sun, reducing the temperature by ten degrees, which Lily welcomed.

She found the thick, slow traffic in Moonstone perfect for self-flagellation over Marcus. He was right. She didn't need him. She could not fall in love with him. She'd known him only a few days. He used rumpled sheets that got washed who knows when. He liked dirt. He preferred the company of a lavender hen over Lily.

Ruth lived near the school southeast of the town square in a white, German-style bungalow with a sturdy front porch that sported a swing. As Lily stepped onto the porch, the roar of a motorcycle stopped her. Her heartbeat stuttered like the engine. Marcus weaved around cars, then cut onto the sidewalk. She should arrest him. But then she'd have to deal with him.

In a moment he stood next to her, wearing clean tan chinos, a blue polo shirt that outlined his physique in a way that made her lips twitch, and--

"Where did you get that badge?" Lily squinted for closer inspection.

"Long time ago. Dad took me to the Cheyenne rodeo. We got the behind-the-scenes tour. They give you this star."

"It says Cheyenne Frontier Days. Don't you think Ruth and the other women are going to notice?"

"Wanna bet?"

She knew the answer to that. "This is all wrong. You can go to jail for impersonating an officer."

"Will you bring me lunch? No more omelets though. Ruby and Raspberry looked mighty sad earlier when I filched their eggs."

Lily whimpered. "Why are you here? You said you wouldn't help me."

"It's going to rain soon. Can't muck around at my dig so I decided to join you for some fun."

Marcus's shrug of sincerity irritated her. Couldn't he have confessed to being jealous of her "boyfriends"? Nothing she said or did had an affect on him. She was starting to get pissed off at herself.

She rang the doorbell. Ruth invited Marcus in for lemonade and cookies. Lily tagged along with her evidence kit.

They settled into a living room bright with photos from Ruth's travels. Marcus said, "You're a professional. A mighty fine one at that."

Ruth, neat and trim in her blue jeans and white camp shirt, grinned as she sat next to him on the cherry red couch. "Thank you. That one's of the Wyoming mountains. I went gold digging there last year. You should go with me next year."

"I love Wyoming."

Lily rolled her eyes. "Isn't this getting hard for you? Aren't you eighty-six?"

"Yes. Two years older than Henri." She sniffled, taking out a handkerchief embroidered in red threads. "I'm sorry. Henri's in danger."

"How so?" Lily sat straighter in the chair across the low table from them.

"His heart. She's going to break it. It's me he's always wanted."

After exchanging a look with Lily, Marcus held Ruth's hand in his. "Any man would be nuts not to want you."

Ruth fluttered her eyelashes at Marcus. He smiled down at her.

Lily wanted to barf. "You said something on Tuesday about a ring he gave you."

Ruth scurried off the sofa to open a drawer in a desk at the end of the room. She toddled back with a gold ring sporting a small white stone. She laid it in Marcus's broad palm.

"That's a moonstone," she said. "We were in grade school when he gave that to me one Christmas. He made me promise we'd always be friends no matter what and always come back to Moonstone at the holiday. Years later, every year that he was Santa, I was his Mrs. Claus."

Tears began to flow down her papery cheeks.

Lily choked, not sure what to say.

Marcus took Ruth's handkerchief and daubed at her tears. He took the ring and slid it onto Ruth's ring finger on her left hand. "Henri's lost, confused. Maybe you're not lost and he needs you to take the lead. Wear the ring, wear the memories, let Henri see what a beauty you are. Maybe he'll finally come to his senses and let his heart come home to you."

Lily's own heart flip-flopped. She wanted to be Ruth, feel the heat of the ring as Marcus slipped it on her own finger. She cleared her throat. "Ruth, could I get your fingerprints?"

Ruth nodded, staring into her moonstone ring with a melancholy twist on her face. "You'll find my prints all over the poison pie plates."

"Why?" Lily asked.

"Did you see the high heels that woman wore? I wasn't about to let her trip in the grass and dump the pies and destroy my moment of victory. I carried them from her car to the table."

Lily found that confusing. Ruth had been nice to her rival? Lily remembered another important aspect. "Why did you use Kirsten's restaurant kitchen to bake your pies?"

"My stove is small and over thirty years old. I wasn't taking a chance of those pies failing."

Minutes later, Lily left Ruth's house with Marcus, not sure what to think. "If she carried Felicity's pies, it could mean she had time to slip something into them."

"Her tears were real."

"But that only proves my point. She really loves Henri. She'd do anything to keep him."

Next, they drove to the Marsh Marigold Motel near the casino a few miles east of Moonstone. Lily regretted that she and Marcus weren't driving together so they could go over the case. But he was right. Somebody might see them together. Gossip wouldn't help her solve the case and keep her job.

The motel consisted of a house flanked by six lodging units on each side, all of them with yellow vinyl siding. Felicity Starr was in Unit Six, just left of the house. As Todd mentioned, she had several suitcases crowding the room, but oddly enough, Lily didn't spot many clothes on hangers. Did she expect to move into the North Pole mansion soon?

Dressed in pink short-shorts and a pink sleeveless top that did good things for her cheeks and dark hair, Felicity led them out her unit's back door to a patio that overlooked Lake Superior. Water sloshed against the dock and piers. Boats banged against their moorings. Thunder argued far off to the west and over the lake; the sun played peek-a-boo yet.

Felicity offered Marcus a cola she grabbed from a cooler on top of a picnic table but ignored Lily, as expected. Marcus sat across from Felicity. Lily remained standing.

The table held red earthenware flower pots sitting on newspapers. Felicity took up her paintbrush to continue decorating them with scenes of the dock and boats. Lily complimented her, then asked her how poison may have gotten into her banana cream pie.

The brush slipped, marring the pot. "I love him. I couldn't do it. Somebody framed me."

"What do you think about Ruth?"

"I don't know. I'd never use conjecture. I never lie or gossip. It's wrong." Felicity handed Marcus her brush while she wiped the smudged paint off the pot with a damp rag.

Lily noted Felicity wasn't looking them in the eyes. "You made the pies here?"

"In the kitchen." Felicity nodded toward the house, continuing her painting. "Mrs. Arneson was kind enough to let me use her kitchen and everything in it. Todd was a great help, too."

"Is Mrs. Arneson home? I'd like permission to look around."

"She's cleaning a unit, but she wouldn't mind. Go on."

"You two must be good friends by now," Lily ventured, wondering if Mrs. Arneson might be a suspect. Maybe she was protective of Felicity and wanted to help her romance along with Henri. A rundown motel could always use an infusion of cash.

"We both love music." Felicity looked up, brown eyes going soft. "I've asked her to play the organ at my wedding."

Marcus asked, "He's proposed?"

"Not yet, but I can feel it coming. These pots are for the table decorations at the reception."

Lily slid onto the bench next to Felicity. "You're so young, why--"

"Why saddle myself with a rich old man? Who could die soon and leave it all to me?"

Lily nodded at the woman's sarcasm. "Something like that."

"He's giving all his money to charity when he dies. I asked him to. I didn't want his money destroying our love. He more than agreed, and we sealed it with more than a kiss."

The gamine's suggestive smile for Marcus sent a blush up his face, surprising Lily. Could it be Marcus flirted as his own defense mechanism? Was there shyness beneath the surface? With sudden clarity--or was it hope?--she suspected he never knew she'd glimpsed him nude that day in her rearview mirror. If she dug down to his inner strata, what would Lily find? She stored the tidbit away for later.

Lily and Marcus went inside for an inspection that yielded nothing out of the ordinary. There were the usual cleaning supplies, plastic canisters of detergent, and mouse traps under the sink. More clear, plastic canisters of flour, sugar, pasta, and canned goods filled the cupboards.

Later, in the parking lot, Marcus said, "There's something odd about her."

"You think she's lying?"

"No, I believe she's sincere. But it's odd for somebody in her twenties to want to marry an old geezer and get nothing out of it. That's the part I don't trust."

"No true love involved?"

"I'd be suspicious. I'm hitting the Internet for some research later. Want me to plug in Felicity's name for you?"

"Yes, thank you. I'll have buddies at the sheriff's department pursue some other lists. But I wonder if we both might save time by starting with the LeBarrons? Wouldn't Henri have hired a detective to check her out? Maybe there's a report already done on her."

"Meet you at the North Pole."

Chapter 5

When they parked outside the mansion in the small, west lot out of sight of the restaurant, Marcus took off his helmet and asked, "Why did you come to Moonstone? You seem like a city gal through and through, like Felicity."

Lily stiffened. Why couldn't he have asked about the boyfriends she'd made up? Nobody but Kirsten knew why she'd taken this job. "I grew up in San Francisco. It was time to stretch."

"Tired of the fog?"

He was playing her. Why did he care?

But why did she care if he knew it all? It might be one way to put a final end to any thoughts of something more between them. "I'm here because my actor brother almost died from meth abuse. He was pegged as the new young Redford. Now he's thrown that all away. He's left rehab and I can't find him. But being in law enforcement gives me a leg up in finding him. This job opened, and here I am."

"A lot on your shoulders." He gripped her upper arm for a fleeting but firm touch of support. Wind caught his hair, fluttering it above eyes that looked as serious as the sky now. "I'm your friend. You're not just here because it's a job. I can see it in your intensity."

A tear slid down her cheek. She slapped at it before it stained her uniform. "While in one of his rehab stints he confessed it all got started when he was introduced to the drugs while here on a fishing trip with buddies."

"I've heard remote rural areas are where the dealers stash their labs. I'll keep an eye out for you."

She drew in a fortifying breath to look up at him, shivering under his supportive gaze. "Marcus, I'm the one who arranged the fishing trip to the famous Brule River. My parents, like a lot of rich people, flew in here for the famous fishing. My brother loved it. I bought him and some pals a trip as a birthday gift. Seems they found more than fish in the woods. I introduced my baby brother to meth."

His face went slack in shock, then he came toward her, but stepped back. She could see that he felt torn as to what to do in public. Take her in his arms or not?

She said, "I met Kirsten in a class in Chicago, where I went for my training, hoping to meet people who at least knew this area and who could help me get a job here. She helped me get my job."

"And you're hoping fate keeps working? That you'll find the bastards who provided your brother with the meth? How dangerous are these people?"

The way his face softened put a lump in her throat. Her insides raced with agitation like the gray clouds overhead. "We better get inside before it pours on us."

He took the rodeo star off his chest. "I wouldn't want Henri to laugh at us. Or at you."

"Thanks."

He'd changed the subject, not pressing her for more about her brother. He'd made a point of respecting her uniform, she realized. She couldn't make too much of it.

It was close to three o'clock and Leonard Moline was serving Henri a snack in the upstairs parlor, a room filled with books, a game table with an onyx chess set, and a collection of clear Steuben glass figurines of fish, fowl, and fauna of the North Woods. Lily wondered about Felicity's goal for these riches. Could Henri really want to give all this to a woman he'd known only days since meeting her at the casino?

Henri sat in a wheelchair at a tray table, about to dig into what looked like a mini version of Kirsten's flower petal omelets.

With a shaky hand, Henri motioned for them to sit in soft, black leather chairs. "Leonard, please bring our fine deputy and this lug something cold to drink. Can't you see they're hard at work trying to pin a murder on me?"

Lily didn't let the man's bluster bother her. "Now why would we want to do that?"

"So you don't blame Felicity. Blame me instead."

Marcus sat forward. "She's a fine woman. She told me she's not marrying you for your money. Must be your personality."

Henri chuckled behind a napkin. "Nah. It's my good looks and vitality. Don't let this wheelchair fool you. The legs get tired, but that's about all."

Lily couldn't help blushing at the exchange, but she didn't want Marcus doing her job for her. "Henri, you and Gigi were friends for how long?"

"Since college days. Gigi was in my wife's class. She thought of her as a daughter. My wife also appreciated the influence Gigi came to wield in the Twin Cities."

Leonard Moline plunked down a tray with lemonade on a nearby table. As he served it Lily asked, "Mr. Moline, I take it you didn't like Gigi much."

Dressed in a navy suit and bow tie today, he said, "I favor not speaking of...the witch...at all."

Lily willed herself not to openly shiver at the chill in the air.

Henri piped up, "Gigi gave my man, Moline, here, a bad review some years ago, putting his Chinese restaurant out of business. My wife heard about it and I hired Leonard. Gigi didn't mean it."

"A Chinese restaurant?" She salivated on the spot, but she also couldn't imagine the dour man cooking Moo Goo Gai Pan. *Moo Goo Guy Moline?*

Marcus asked, "So you're happy that Gigi's no longer with us?"

Leonard marched from the room. Talk about drawing suspicion to himself. Marcus's hiked eyebrows said he concurred. But Leonard's open reaction probably also meant he didn't commit any crimes.

She asked Henri, "Why do you love Felicity?"

He held up a forkful of the flower omelet. "This is called the Crystal, in honor of the first-grade teacher who's marrying my son, Peter. She planted the flowers out back of the mansion in honor of my deceased wife earlier this summer, and now we're eating the blossoms. Felicity suggested we start naming the flower dishes after people we like. She says flowers are what the soul rests on when it gets tired." He winked. "Don't you think she's the loveliest of gals?"

Marcus said, "So you're eating soul food?"

Henri, munching, scowled at Marcus.

Lily swallowed a giggle, enjoying Marcus's joke. "Have you hired a private detective to check her out?"

"Heavens, no!" Henri shrugged around another bite of omelet.

"What did she do before coming here?"

"This and that. Besides, have you ever seen her dance? Makes a man forget to ask a lot of things. At my age, I don't have time for a lot of questions. And the answers don't always matter."

Once outside, Lily bit her lip in thought. "Why would Henri take a stranger's word for who she is?"

"Love is blind," said Marcus, putting on his helmet as if it were a punctuation mark. He mounted his bike.

Love is blind. He said it so blithely that it made Lily wonder if love didn't matter to him at this point in his life. As his motorcycle roared away into traffic, the loneliness she'd had out at Tootsie's farm crept across her again. If only she could find her brother--find some link here in Moonstone, find the people who had become his drug buddies--the loneliness might finally go away.

Marcus had mentioned that he was going back to his RV before the storm hit to work on notes from his dig, so Lily took advantage of that and drove out to Tootsie Winters' place.

After parking her Honda near the chicken pen, Lily slipped rubber boots over her polished shoes. Instead of marching to the house, she popped open an umbrella and paused to look at the hens under the bench. What was it about these animals that had Marcus bonding with them? The hens had created a blue, buff, red, and white wall around Lulu, protecting her from the sprinkles.

"Hey, gals," Lily said, looking around to see if Tootsie or anybody else might overhear her talking to chickens. "What is it you like about the guy? And why does he like you? How do I make him like me?"

She imagined the answer automatically. Out here in the woods, who wouldn't want a guy for company, protecting you from wolves and coyotes? Hadn't Tootsie mentioned the same thing, needing protection when her husband, Bob, was away working on the cruise boat?

It struck Lily that this was what Felicity felt with Henri--protected.

Did it work the other way, too? Did Marcus enjoy the company of chickens out here? Did a man need a woman in that way? Was he lonely, too?

A flame came alive inside Lily's heart, but she dared not believe Marcus might need her company in that way. But did Henri need Felicity because he was lonely? Was life with Leonard Moline getting tiresome? Was he not to be trusted? He certainly wasn't snuggly. But how did it all add up to murder? Surely Leonard would realize that murdering Gigi would end his association with the LeBarrons, thus ending his cushy lifestyle. That was, if he got caught.

A chill whipped around Lily. Rain spattered her pants. She hurried to the yellow farmhouse. The one person who could confirm such a theory based only on a tiny threadbare piece of gossip was Tootsie Winters.

Tootsie opened the door, squinting. "What now?"

Lily decided to try a new tack with the woman. "That is the loveliest outfit, Tootsie. It shows off your prominent cheekbones." The garish lime-green cotton tent dress had butterflies embroidered across the bodice. Its straps exposed Tootsie's fleshy upper arms and shoulders. When Tootsie moved, her breasts bobbed about, obviously unleashed from a bra, making the butterflies look in flight.

"Why, thank you, Deputy. You're the first to see my new creation."

"You sew, too? You're talented way beyond reason. Marcus says you're an excellent cook, too."

"Marcus did?" While patting her short, silver hair, Tootsie led her into a roomy farm kitchen. She indicated a chair at a walnut table with homemade placemats made of knitted pink yarn. "Please sit down. I made a batch of peanut butter cookies for Marcus. I'll get you a glass of milk. You can taste-test."

Lily recalled salted nut rolls in Marcus's cooler. He loved peanuts. She'd have to bring him some and see how he reacted. "You seem to have changed your tune about Marcus."

"Not at all. I want him gone."

That gave Lily whiplash. "So why make him cookies?" *Unless they contain poison?*

Rain plinked at the kitchen window above the sink while Tootsie set down a plate of warm cookies.

"Honey," she said, "I'm playing nice with him because I'm trying to figure him out. I'm pretty sure he's not a paleontologist. He uses a big shovel. Don't those people use delicate tools like toothbrushes so they don't ruin the bones they find? Don't they usually have graduate students helping them?"

Damn but she was good. Lily chewed on her cookie. "You've confronted him with this?"

Tootsie poured milk for them. "And make him mad so he murders me, or harms my silkies?"

The thought of Marcus being a fake so disturbed Lily that she skipped asking Tootsie about Leonard Moline.

All the way back to Moonstone in a thunderous storm with lightning the color of Lulu fracturing the clouds, Lily tried to argue away Tootsie's logic. But Marcus digging for days with only a shovel did appear suspicious.

She did the obvious. She called the University of Wisconsin in Madison to inquire about him. The communications officer told her nobody by the name of Marcus Linden worked there.

Marcus Linden had betrayed her.

When she got back to her office, Todd noticed her slamming file drawers. "You mad about my paint job?"

She wilted into her desk chair, her head matching the storm bang for bang. "I'm sorry." He gave her a pitiful, puppy-dog grin. She looked about the old store. All the walls sported a new, sky blue patina instead of the dingy beige. "You did all of this since I've been gone this morning?"

"Yeah. And guess what?" He bounced on his toes.

His eager enthusiasm made her grin. She needed Todd's goofiness right now. "What?"

"Caught five more mice in traps. I'll bring over the poison and we'll get the sneaky ones. You want the basement painted, too?"

"Can you do it before Wednesday? My boss is coming."

"Dick-head Hollandale?"

"How do you know his name? And it's not dick-head. It's Sheriff Richard Hollandale."

The teen hooked a hip on the corner of her desk. "Coupla newspaper reporters stopped by and I heard them call him a dick-head."

Lily plunked her forehead into her hands for a massage. "You talked to reporters?"

"Yeah, sure, to cover for you. They asked what you were like. Told 'em you were a perfectionist, liked to iron your uniform and do your nails. They wrote that all down. I could tell they respect you."

The tapping on the roof was not the rain. It was the proverbial nails in her coffin. "You told them I like to iron?"

"Don't you?"

"How do you know I iron?"

"I was early one day last week and was at your kitchen door. I saw you through the window. But you were still in your pajamas so I left."

Lily didn't know where to begin, so she let it all go, except for the disrespect of her desk. "Don't sit on my desk, okay?"

"Okay, Dep."

To avoid the reporters she could see camped about Moonstone's square, she got in her car and headed out of Moonstone close to six that Sunday night. The rain had lifted. With it drenching the red dirt fire lanes, tracks would be easy to see. But if the sun came out, even late like this, the red dirt and sand would be dry within the half-hour.

She let the car follow its nose down country roads. She stopped--holster on her belt--at every hunting shack, every abandoned cabin, every suspicious spot where a meth lab might be set up. By seven, with the sun sinking behind the tall pines, she'd scoured a few square miles. She tried to pretend she was doing this for Jase, but the image of Marcus stared at her from the roadside shadows. Why had he lied to her? Who was he? Had her parents sent her a bodyguard? Or was he some rich bachelor being paid by them to tease her away from this job?

Worse yet, was he a law officer? Had Dick-head Hollandale sent out an undercover officer? Did the department already know about something out in the woods behind the Winters' place?

A biting speech had begun forming in her head. She drove out to the Brule River to demand answers.

But Marcus's white RV was gone.

Lily let herself into her upstairs apartment, telling herself good riddance to whoever he was. She grabbed a cola, then headed to the bathroom to wash up.

She dropped the soda; it exploded as she pulled her gun at the sight of the man amid bubbles in her bathtub. "What the hell are you doing here? Better yet, who are you?"

"Marcus Linden."

"No, you're not. Tootsie's on to you. I also called the university." She kept the gun trained on him. Her forehead went hot, but her training came to the fore to keep her breathing steady.

"I was just hired. Probably not on any directory lists yet. All the better. Less spam email."

"I thought you went to college in Madison."

"You assumed." He swabbed behind his ears with a designer wash cloth her mother had sent her. "Minnesota. But I'm from Madison. Didn't you do some sort of 411 or Internet search on me by now?"

Triple crap. She hadn't. She exchanged her gun for her cell phone. "Don't you move. Hands above the bubbles."

He complied.

Before she could stop the information operator, Lily had been put through to a groggy woman. After a brief conversation, Lily stuffed the phone back in its holster on her belt.

"Well?" he asked, plunking his bare feet through the bubbles to rest them on the end of the claw-footed tub.

Lily wanted to run and hide. "I think I woke up your mother."

He laughed heartily, splashing soap suds into the cola pool on the floor. "Wait until I tell her I'm dating a deputy sheriff."

"We're not dating. Why the heck would you tell her that?"

"For the purposes of keeping my mother happy, we're dating. She'd disown me if I were doing one-night stands. Not respectful of the woman, she always said. Always, she said I had to have at least two dates before I let the girl down, and I had to let her down easy, had to say it was my fault, my flaw."

Now this piqued Lily's interest. She sank against the doorjamb. "And what flaws might you have?"

"I've tried a few, actually. I look at flaws as something we can buy into, or discard on our own personal rummage sale of life." He leaned back in the tub to stare at the ceiling. A bubble iceberg floated over his submerged chest. "I told some that I can't afford to date. Now there's a quick turnoff. One summer I stopped wearing deodorant to see how that might work. It worked."

Lily shook her head in disgust. "What about the flaw called conceit?"

He sat up, shaping the bubbles into peaks across the tub like pie meringue. "Don't mistake content with conceit. I like my life. I'm contented."

The insinuation niggled her. "I'm very contented, too."

"That's great because I talked with Todd. It seems he told some reporters I was helping you."

"You are undercover."

"No. I said 'helping'. I distinctly said *you* had asked for my help. Which is true. You needed me."

Thinking about how this would look in the newspaper, Lily planted her butt on the toilet lid, with her head in her hands.

Marcus sloshed about. "Listen, I'll call the reporters and tell them you fired me, then I'll call Mom and tell her we broke up. She'll be pleased she doesn't have to come with bail money this time."

She peeked at him between splayed fingers over her face. "You've been arrested in the past? I've been working with a criminal?" Now who was the dick-head?

"Paleontologists poke around in places. People get nervous and call the cops."

She'd witnessed that, but there was that other fatal flaw... "You still live with your mother?"

"Hey, I'm not over thirty yet. But tell you what, soon as I turn thirty next spring, I'll move in here. Big boy stuff."

"Very funny. Now get out."

"I need a towel." He rose out of the water, stepping out of the tub, nude right in front of her, bubbles sliding off the end of his naughty parts.

"Don't be disgusting," she gasped, turning around.

He reached for the fluffy, white, pristine designer towel on her rack. "What's disgusting is you believing Tootsie over me. You also pulled a gun on me. Aren't you ever off-duty?"

"Not when I have a nude man in my apartment. I have to report you."

"How's that going to look in the headline? 'Nude man in new deputy's bathtub'." He had the towel wrapped over his vitals. Soap bubbles stuck to his chin and chest.

"So I'm off-duty now. I'm a woman being accosted who's about to call 911."

"Let's make it look good then."

He scooped her up then set her down with a splash in the tub of soap suds.

She spit out bitter suds. "Look at my uniform."

"That's all I look at."

"What's that supposed to mean?" He wanted her out of the uniform? Fat chance.

Marcus was mopping up the floor with several designer towels he'd found in her linen closet. The cola would likely ruin them. "You didn't even notice the tub."

She sloshed the bubbles aside. The tub was sparkling white. "How'd you get the stains out?"

"Todd told me about this super rust remover stuff."

"Todd was here? He doesn't have a key." She climbed out on a towel he set down for her. Her uniform, leather belt, and leather shoes were ruined.

"He was vacuuming your living room. Anyway, I headed over to the hardware store, got the stuff and ordered you a new water conditioner. Then I decided to take advantage of the tub. I haven't had a good bath in a month."

"What about your precious river?"

"I don't like to use soap. The trout wouldn't like it."

She pointed at the tub. "Drain your filth, please." She looked down at herself. Any lab report would tell her she had Marcus's essence all over her. Their skin cells had commingled in the water. Instead of shivering, the notion made her heat up. Couldn't he make at least a modicum of an advance on her, pretend he wanted to help her undress out of her wet clothes?

Of course Marcus was instead cleaning the splashed cola off the ceiling.

"I can do the rest." She wanted him out of the tiny room, out of her apartment before her body's heat index called for climbing into her refrigerator.

"Yeah," he said, wiping the wall next to the toilet, "you can take care of yourself. That's why you ended up in a bathtub."

"That's not fair. You manhandled me."

He swabbed cola off the sink. She took a perverse pleasure in watching him ruin her mother's designer washcloth. "What'd you do before becoming a cop?" he asked.

"I suppose you're insinuating I should go back to whatever that was." His shrug made her mood grow darker. "Commercials. My parents are in the industry. They got me gigs. They had hopes of my going into acting."

"You're pretty enough for it. Why not?"

She took off her squishy shoes. "Because they wanted it for me. I also hated it. I hated all the fussing. For one commercial it took six people to dress me. And it was a hand cream commercial."

His deep-throated laugh made it okay for her to smile, too. There was a sober truth behind it all though. "My brother had the real acting bug. But last time I saw him he had rotted teeth and gums. His face was a mess of pimply scars from meth use."

Marcus sat down on the stool lid. "So big sister's going to stay in Moonstone until she roots out the evil lurking in the woods even if it takes her forever."

She sensed he was driving to some point. "I'm committed to payback. You're committed to...what? Digging up beaver bones?"

She left the confines of the bathroom, finally able to breathe in her bedroom with the door closed between them. She leaned against the back of the door, unbuttoning her wet uniform shirt. She yearned to wash it and iron it, to muster up the calming feeling of setting her life straight again like the creases on her sleeves.

Marcus talked through the door. "I like my job. I really am a paleontologist. Ever since I was a kid I wanted to dig up dinosaurs, to touch the past. Everything's connected. I like thinking about how the past might help us predict the future. It's crazy cosmic stuff, but I'm committed to it. What about you? What'd you want to do when you were a kid?"

Lily slipped out of her wet pants, then hurried to change underwear. "I wanted to play in an orchestra and the band."

When he didn't laugh from the other side of the door, she added, "Music was my thing, but mom and dad didn't want me playing the clarinet."

"Why not?"

She slipped into tan shorts and her cleaned and ironed Green Bay Packer t-shirt. "They were afraid it would make me buck-toothed."

"Why music?"

She sat on the bed, stunned. She'd never had a conversation with anybody about her passions, not even with Kirsten. Through the safety of her bedroom door, she said, "I liked the uniforms." He didn't laugh yet, so she went on. "I dreamed of being in a marching band, with uniforms with snappy epaulets and brass buttons, and being in the orchestra with the crisp white blouses and black skirts on all the women. I would see rows of clarinets, everybody in unison...a family of clarinets, everybody following the same music. I dreamed of being part of them, of playing my clarinet in the high school band in the Rose Bowl Parade. That's the only time I really wanted to be on television. Not for hand cream commercials."

When he didn't answer, she asked, "You there yet?" Maybe she'd spooked him.

"Oh yeah."

"You decent?" There were always his tricks.

"Oh yeah."

He was relaxing in her living room chair with the green leaf pattern, looking as enticing as ever with a black t-shirt stretched across his shoulders and chest, and denim jeans. He was barefoot, which made things feel intimate to Lily. She'd slipped on loafers.

Still suspicious, she asked, "Why are you here? Besides the bath?"

"I think there is something going on out in the woods near my camping area."

Her heart quickened. "You saw something?"

"No, but I smelled something odd before I left, a fire, something odd on the wind like chemicals. I thought it best to move on instead of playing detective."

"That's smart." She rushed to the kitchen for a fresh cola for both of them. "So how far away do you think they were?"

"I haven't a clue. Like I said, I left pretty fast." Her disappointment seemed to affect him because he added with great earnestness, "I think Ruth knows more about Felicity than she's letting on."

She set down the colas on the table next to him. "Like what?"

"Not sure."

"Did you go online yet?"

"Didn't have time yet," he said.

"Let's do some digging."

She led him downstairs. Todd had hooked up the new computer on her desk. Marcus commented on the fresh, blue paint in the place.

"Todd did that, too," she said.

"You realize that kid's smitten with you."

"Jealous?"

"Nah. Remember? We broke up. It's going to be in all the papers."

She was resigned to their relationship being one in which he told jokes and she tolerated them.

Lily focused on the computer screen. It gave her solid answers. But not the ones she expected. A quick search on the Internet made them both sit back.

Marcus whistled. "Felicity Starr is a nun?"

Lily squinted hard at the screen. She clicked to enlarge the image. "She looks good in a habit."

"Sexiest damn nun I've ever encountered."

"I wonder if Henri knows."

"I wonder if Ruth knows. I bet she does, but why didn't she tell us? I had my best blue shirt on and my badge."

"Leave your rodeo star off this time. We're getting serious."

Chapter 6

Ruth was still up when Lily knocked. After Marcus and Lily stepped inside, Lily got to the point. "Why are you protecting Felicity?"

Ruth led them to her living room where she poured them raspberry tea over ice. "I want to protect Santa Claus. He's going to become a laughingstock."

"Santa, the Saint, and the Sinner? But who's who, Ruth? Have you been lying?" Lily sat forward in her chair to skewer Ruth with a look.

It worked. "All right. When I happened across Felicity in his bed that day, I saw a light in Henri's eyes that he never had before, not even for his wife and he loved her dearly. I can't make him feel younger, but Felicity does. Because I love him, I decided to change my thinking on her."

"Mighty generous," Lily said, sipping the icy tea, wondering if it were poisonous.

Marcus asked of Ruth, "Does he know she's a nun? That her charity is her convent?"

Ruth sank even lower on the red sofa cushion. "Religious orders can't get young women to commit anymore. Her convent is now a retirement home for aging nuns. But what Henri doesn't know is she can't cook or bake worth a lick. Felicity's the one who's been lying." Ruth's hand shook when lifting the glass of tea.

Lily asked, "Did you do more than help Lily carry her pies that day?"

"Did I make her pies for her? No. That was Leonard."

"Henri's assistant?" Lily took a slug of raspberry tea. Did Leonard frame Felicity after all? Or was Leonard being set up? By Ruth?

Marcus was no help. He looked as confused as Lily as he topped off the tea glasses.

"Henri needs Leonard." Ruth's face pinched toward tears. "Please don't tell Henri where you heard this."

"Ruth, I can't guarantee this won't come out. I'm sorry." Lily ached for the elderly woman so in love and watching it slip away.

Ruth sniffled. "While I was making my pies in Kirsten's restaurant kitchen, Leonard came in asking for the ingredients for banana cream pie. He said...that he needed to make...a 'final gesture'."

Lily and Marcus sat back in unison, sharing the obvious conclusion. Lily asked, "How final?"

Ruth's tears flowed. "I don't know. Please help me. All of this scares me. Henri doesn't deserve any of this."

❧

Lily couldn't sleep that night. *"Please help me."* The plea of an innocent woman scared for the man she loved? Or a cover-up?

She got up several times to look at Marcus's RV parked behind her building. A light burned behind the closed mini-blinds. He couldn't sleep either. Lily again thought about the issue that was primal between men and women: needing each other. But how much? How much was dangerous? Ruth had sensed danger to her heart, or so she'd let on. She'd given up Henri. But Lily hadn't missed the pain left behind with that decision to go it alone. Could a woman really give up the man she loved?

On Labor Day morning, Lily woke to less humidity, sunshine flowing in from the street side windows, cardinals trilling outside, and the realization that she'd overslept. She shot from bed to pull on a fresh uniform. She pulled her hair back into a ponytail, then decided to make coffee for Marcus so they could discuss the case. When she peered out the kitchen window, though, the RV was gone.

Dull fatigue tugged at her. Facing the reporters, traffic, tourists, and the heat held no appeal. But the memory of Jase on stage at fourteen, the same age as Todd and full of promise, revived her. When Jase had been inside a role--facing the spotlight and the heat of reviews--he didn't break. She couldn't either.

Then she remembered Marcus had mentioned she had an "intensity". That made her smile and drink her coffee with gusto. Somehow her strength would reach Jason wherever he was and return him to his old self, maybe even bring him home. She heard once that the effects of a butterfly's wings whispering into the air could be felt around the world. If true, then her strength--her actions--could make it to Jase.

She decided to talk again to Henri LeBarron that Monday morning. She suspected he hadn't yet shared all his wisdom on his girlfriends, or about Leonard. Fortunately, creepy Leonard had gone shopping in Superior.

Henri insisted on shuffling with his walker about his long living room for exercise while they talked. "Gotta get in shape to walk my bride down the aisle." He looked robust, with color in his face, his white hair combed as if expecting the wedding to be that day. Felicity seemed good for him.

Lily followed him back and forth, focusing on the intricate colors of the Oriental carpet. After getting niceties out of the way, she asked Henri about Leonard and the meaning of the "final gesture".

Henri guffawed. "Leonard wanted to shame Felicity into leaving me, give her a nudge to leave town. I'm afraid Leonard's been used to only the two of us for too many years. But Felicity's a scrapper. She got upset and tossed flour on him. He didn't like having to take his suit to the cleaners."

Lily grinned at the vision of "Lincoln" covered with flour. "So she made her own pies after all." That brought a sobering thought. "Henri, could Felicity have wanted to get rid of Gigi to get on Leonard's good side?"

Henri stopped shuffling. The light stayed in his eyes. "She lives by the Lord's rules. What do you think?"

People in prison also said they lived by the Lord's rules, so that didn't sway Lily. But after she stepped outside the North Pole mansion, she concluded she was back to having nothing on the case but one fact: Somebody put poison in the pies.

Dejected, she headed to her car parked in the small lot carved out of the lawn next to the mansion. As she opened her car door, the world spun upside down.

Her forehead hit the steering wheel hard before she fell backwards with her throbbing head doing a freefall onto the blacktop.

"Hey, Dep? You okay?"

Lily couldn't even groan, her head hurt that much. But looking up into the panicked look on Todd's face forced her to nudge onto her elbows. A washcloth fell off her forehead. Todd picked it up.

"Mr. Moline brought you this. You feeling better?"

"Was I out cold?" She looked around. Nobody had gathered, a good thing.

"Yeah, but I think just a couple minutes. I was coming over to get a sandwich and there you were, laid out flat like road kill." Todd handed her cap to her.

Gingerly, she slipped it on. The stars were dissipating. She felt around her forehead and the back of her head, but didn't find any knots. "Just you and Leonard saw me?"

So where was Leonard now? There was something odd about being out here alone, falling, and in a jiffy Leonard was there with a cooling cloth for her head.

"Don't be embarrassed, Dep. We'll never tell. Maybe you need some of that black coffee you always drink. Maybe you're tired and slipped or something."

Or something, all right. She wanted to talk with Leonard. If he were being shoved aside from a cushy lifestyle, he could still be planning a "final gesture" for Felicity. Or Lily?

The fear that there could soon be a second murder on her hands shot a tingle through Lily.

"Want me to drive ya back to the office?" Todd gave her a hand up.

She brushed herself off but could see she'd need to change to a clean uniform. Oil spots from the hot blacktop stained her pants and probably her entire backside.

"I'll handle the driving," she said, but when he let go of her she bent with the breeze. She slapped a hand onto the car to steady herself. "You can come along though." His chatter would keep her focused.

Fortunately, they only had to go around the square. She parked behind her building.

A little past noon, while she was standing in a pair of shorts and her Green Bay Packer t-shirt ironing a fresh uniform, she got a loud knock on the back kitchen door.

It was Marcus with a large bag. He rushed in. "What the hell happened? Kirsten caught up with me after Todd told her about saving you."

"He didn't save me. I'm fine." Her head still ached, but the sight of him in her kitchen was like an elixir because she could switch her focus to him rather than her pain. His wavy hair hung mussed from his rush. He wore a fresh blue shirt and tan shorts, but it was the worry on his face that endeared her. "You really worried about me?"

"Yeah, because you didn't bring me my lunch out at the chicken farm. I'm starved."

She should've known he'd negate any romance she was hoping for with a joke. She returned to ironing.

He took the food out of the bag and set things on the table. Lily's mouth watered at the smell of garlic and chicken. But Marcus wrinkled his nose. "She might be trying to make Chinese food."

Kirsten laughed. "Finally."

"I prefer Mexican and Italian, but then, you're the permanent resident here. You're stuck with this stuff."

She paused in her ironing. "That's right. You're leaving soon for classes in Madison?"

"Mine don't start until Wednesday. I've got tomorrow. Now tell me what happened."

"I slipped is all. Maybe on the hot tar in the blacktop. Bumped my head a little."

"Todd thinks Moline might've tried to murder you."

The "final gesture"? Her instincts hummed. "Did Todd see him do something?"

Marcus munched on a bite of something from the Styrofoam box. "He didn't say so. He just doesn't like Leonard. Neither do I. Maybe I should hang around, keep an eye out for you."

She'd give anything to have her very own paleontologist at her side all the time, but this one didn't seem to notice that her heart couldn't take it. She refused to give herself false hope with Marcus.

"Marcus, I can handle this."

"You'll be more careful?"

Tears poked at the back of her eyes. "I'll be careful."

"Okay." He munched another bite. "This stuff isn't bad, but it needs ketchup or something."

"Don't you dare tell Kirsten that!"

They both laughed.

Later that Monday afternoon, Lily decided to speak to Leonard point-blank. Maybe she could shame the guy into confessing to everything. But the darn man was gone again on an errand.

She went to Ruth's place, thinking the long-time resident would have more information about Leonard. But Ruth was gone.

When Lily drove over to Port Cliff and the Marsh Marigold Motel, she discovered Felicity packing her car. The young woman was crying.

"Felicity, what's the matter?"

"I'm going back to Illinois. All this trouble is because of me. I can't do that to Henri."

"You're giving up? But you love him." Or was that a lie after all?

"This pie contest was the dumbest thing I've ever done. If I had said 'no' none of this would've happened. If I marry Henri he's going to think about the weird connections of events, how it all started with me. What kind of marriage would that be for him?"

Felicity kept packing, but something she said hatched a clue inside Lily. "Felicity, can you stay around for a day or so? I think I can clear all this up. Please?"

The woman finally nodded.

Lily drove back to her office, made notes before she forgot the complicated thread of things zooming through her achy head, then decided she had to share them with Marcus. She had to be sure she wasn't coming at her conclusions about the case with a fuzzy brain.

She drove out to Tootsie's place that afternoon, but didn't find Marcus. Tootsie hurried out her front door, arms flapping. "Did you find Marcus?"

"Why?"

"Todd called here to say he overheard some kids talking about a meth lab out in the woods. Todd's chasing it down. I think he stole a car. When I told Marcus, he shot out of here on his motorcycle."

"That fool kid. I should've known."

"Should've known what?"

"I'll tell you later, Tootsie."

Lily's heart banged hard against her chest wall as she drove for the place where Marcus parked his RV next to the Brule River. Marcus had smelled something there earlier and had moved away for safety's sake. It could be the meth lab Todd was now tracking down.

She was a couple of roads away from the spot among the tall pines when she came across Marcus's motorcycle on its side in a weedy, dusty ditch. She slammed to a stop, sending up a cloud of red dirt she had to wait out before getting out of the car.

"Marcus?"

He'd been thrown a few yards up the way in the tall grass. She found him trying to sit up, rubbing his head. "Boy, there's a lot of this going around," he moaned.

When she helped him, her hand on his back came up smeared with blood. "No, Marcus, this isn't just a bump on the head. You've been shot."

Chapter 7

"Find Todd," he said, spitting out red dirt. "I was catching up to him."

"You sit still while I get my first aid kit."

The bullet had grazed his right shoulder blade, searing a red stripe in his flesh about six inches long. "You're going to have a nasty scar," she said, putting a patch over his wound with shaky fingers. Her heartbeat wouldn't settle down. He'd come close to being killed. She also panicked about Todd. A flickering vision of her brother assailed her.

"What was Todd thinking? He's a good kid. Why the heck wouldn't he have called me?" She inspected a goose egg erupting on the side of his head.

"He tried."

"I had my phone off while talking with Felicity. Todd should know better, though."

"Todd's in love with you."

"Oh not that tripe again."

"Are you blind to the ways of all men, old and young? He has to prove his love to you. Men have to prove stuff."

"Prove his love? He's out here trying to get himself killed to prove--"

His words further cemented what she'd been thinking about earlier. The idea came alive with the force of fireworks in her brain. She kissed Marcus hard on the lips, nibbling, her tongue tasting the dirt, enjoying every moment of knowing he was alive. "Thank you."

"For what?"

"For taking a bullet for me. For pointing me to the answers about Gigi's death."

"Todd did it?"

"No. Now get in my car and don't bleed all over everything. We've got to find Todd."

She called for backup as she and Marcus followed fresh dust kicked up onto the lower branches of pine trees. About two miles east they found an abandoned car with keys still in it.

Lily told Marcus, "You stay put. Lock the doors. Stay down so they can't see you."

"Like hell."

He followed her into the woods which disintegrated into a tangled mess of sumac, scratchy berry vines, and uneven ground from old stumps.

A trail of broken branches led Lily on. She snapped open her holster. "Hey! It's Deputy Schuster. Sheriff's department. Stay where you are."

Scuffling and grunts ensued, replaced by more branches crashing in the woods. Lily pushed on.

Marcus said, "The sons-a-bitches are getting away."

"I'll catch up with them. You stay here."

"No way."

She rushed toward a small, camouflaged tent up ahead and found Todd lying on his back in the pine needles. She slid to her knees next to him, sickened by his bruises, cuts, and torn clothing. "Hey, buddy, it's my turn. You there?"

His eyes popped open. "Did ya get 'em?"

"Never mind. How are you? I'll call an ambulance."

Marcus grabbed her phone to call.

Todd sucked in a deep breath. "I'm okay. Had the wind knocked out of me is all. But I busted a nose. It was really cool how blood spurted all over the place. You proud of me, Dep?"

Lily winced. "Don't you dare move, kid."

Lily took off through the wicked brush. She was scratched up, sweating, almost out of breath before she saw two figures trip over a log several yards ahead. "Hey, stop right there."

They scrambled up and ran harder, branches bashing at them, swallowing them up.

"Crap," she muttered, scrambling harder through the woods. Where was a bear when she needed one?

She got lucky. She found a kid of maybe sixteen with a bloody nose hung up in berry bushes within a couple hundred yards. She left him to go after his buddy who was on all fours diving over a log to hide. She dove right after him, slinging an arm fast around his neck to gag him while pulling one of his arms back fast. He went face first into soft woodland floor, the thick green moss providing an effective gag.

He was bigger than his buddy, but Lily managed a hearty, "You move, and I taser you." He didn't have to know she didn't carry one. She handcuffed him, then sat back to catch her breath before hiking back to rip his buddy out of the berry branches. To her relief, Marcus had caught up to that perp and was staring him down.

Marcus said, "Wow," as he watched her handcuff the guy in the berry thorns.

"What wow?" she said, still trying to catch a breath. She shoved the two teens up the trail ahead of them.

"You watch me doing my job all the time. I've never watched you in action. You're good. Just like on TV."

Just what cops didn't want to hear. But she liked the way Marcus held a soft gaze on her. He didn't wink or joke. This side of Marcus she hadn't seen much of before. It made her heart leap into her throat. She managed to mumble a "Thanks" as they walked on to collect Todd, then got everybody in the squad car that showed up from the neighboring town.

Their private moment stayed with her all the way back to Moonstone. There was something freeing about the gritty dirt kiss with Marcus and going through the trauma with him that she couldn't quite put her finger on. She had no time to worry it to death, though, because she had to take care of the matter of Gigi's death. Lily talked with the DCI officials in Madison and the local district attorney about her new suspicions. They agreed with her next move: invite all the major suspects to the Marsh Marigold Motel near Port Cliff later that evening.

That gave her time to change into her last clean uniform. She went to the mouse-infested basement to start her washer. A dead mouse lay not a foot from the machine. This one had maggots. *Todd would love this*, she thought. She knew enough to know maggots came from flies laying their eggs. She looked around. Sure enough, a basement window was open. It had no screen. Who would want to sneak into her office and apartment? Just about every suspect in Gigi's death.

She went outside. The footprint was unmistakable and only confirmed her suspicions.

At around six that Labor Day, the assistant DA and Lily's major suspects stood in Mrs. Arneson's kitchen in the Marsh Marigold Motel.

Lily opened all the cupboards high and low so the small crowd had full view of ingredients for pies. She noticed Todd leaning against a doorjamb behind the crowd. Her heart held a dull ache for him. He looked exhausted, besides being bruised.

She flicked a glance to Marcus, who stood near the other door. He had no idea what she was going to say. She'd been careful not to involve him in this part.

"Mrs. Arneson, is this pretty much how your kitchen looks all the time?"

The pale woman nodded from her seat at the table.

"Good. Felicity, where did you make your pies?"

The petite woman in her sunny yellow dress pointed to the left of the sink.

Lily said, "By now we know you know you needed some help baking. Who helped you?"

"Nobody. Todd told me to use whatever I wanted and I went to it."

Lily saw Todd grimace. "Todd? You were in a hurry so you didn't help Felicity much, did you? You were in a hurry to get to my place. With what?"

All eyes landed on the teenager.

Todd looked at the floor and mumbled, "Rat poison."

Ruth, seated at the table, groaned, "Oh no."

How many others had already guessed what happened?

Lily continued speaking to Mrs. Arneson. "I noticed you keep a lot of poisons under the sink, but no boxes of rat poison. That's because with all the humidity in summer, you put it into a plastic canister so it doesn't mold."

Lily took out a canister from under the sink. "This one's marked as rat poison, but I'm betting the day Felicity made her pies, it wasn't."

Lily switched her gaze to Todd. "You were filling it fresh, and hadn't yet labeled it, right, Todd? You were preparing to bring me a gift of it for my basement."

Todd nodded, his face transformed to stone. His mother started sniffling.

Lily looked over at Henri, who was in his wheelchair with Felicity standing behind him. "Henri told me that Leonard got doused with flour when he was here. True, Felicity?"

"Yes. I'm sorry." Felicity was looking sickly now, too, as the conclusion became obvious.

Lily filled in the blanks. "Todd got the poison out after Felicity used up her flour on Leonard. But Todd got distracted."

Mrs. Arneson spoke up amid choking tears. "It's my fault. I needed Todd to come help me quick move a dresser and mirror so I could clean behind it."

"And when he got back to the kitchen," Lily noted, "Felicity didn't realize that what she was using to make the pie crusts and fillings amounted to rat poison. I'm betting there were bulk cleaning supplies that had been poured in a jar that looked like vinegar or some other ingredient."

Felicity's knees gave out. Marcus caught her. Ruth got up to give Felicity her chair.

Lily opened the plastic canister and showed everybody the rat poison. "This variety looks like grain. It could be wheat flour, coarsely ground. And with the canister not labeled, Felicity thought it was flour.

"Gigi's death was purely an accident that came about through a chain of events based on how everybody in this town was trying to help the other one. Leonard did what he did because he likes Henri."

Leonard grimaced, his face sallow in the kitchen light.

Lily continued. "Felicity showed her love for Henri by tossing the flour on Leonard. Henri, you were upset with Felicity at the park because you had wanted her to make her pies at the mansion, and if so, this wouldn't have happened."

Lily stopped to collect her strength, to keep her intensity, as Marcus put it. "Todd wanted to impress me because he had a crush on me. But Todd, you even hit me over the head, didn't you, so that you could play hero? But you also wanted to make up for this rat poison mistake, didn't you? So you stole a car to catch criminals for me. You didn't count on them having guns and shooting at you or Marcus."

Mrs. Arneson wailed into her hands.

Todd withered, sliding into a chair.

Lily said, "You opened the basement window, too. You were sneaking inside, doing things for me. Marcus said he caught you vacuuming my apartment. You pretended you had a key, didn't you?"

Todd offered only a slight nod, his chin solidly on his chest.

"Mrs. Arneson, you had no idea that Todd's helping you could have deadly consequences. Had I paid more attention to Todd wanting to clean up my building and rid it of mice, I might have bought the poison myself at the hardware store and he wouldn't have needed to bring it from here. I'm sorry, everybody."

Ruth said, "But why be sorry, dear, when you did a brilliant job of deducing all this?"

"*Barely* deduced it. It took a hit on my head, a kid putting himself in danger for me, and an innocent bystander getting shot for me to see what was going on. I wasn't on my toes like I should've been." Lily took a last fortifying breath, looking at the room of eyes staring back. "Because of my mistakes, I'm offering my resignation."

When she looked toward the door, she saw only Marcus's back as he slipped away.

Chapter 8

When Lily caught up with Marcus outside the Marsh Marigold Motel, she saw disappointment in his face. She said, "I have to quit."

"You did a good job from what I saw. I told you that."

"Moonstone deserves somebody more mature."

"So you're heading back to San Francisco?"

Lily's gut hardened. She hadn't thought that far. "I suppose I'm heading back."

He put on his helmet. "I call it going backward."

"What does that mean?"

"Tell me, what are your hopes and dreams? And don't tell me about the brother. He's gonna take care of himself, no matter what you do. What about your dreams?"

Lily discovered in that moment that she'd been reacting to her parents' wants and her brother's wants for so long that she'd perhaps forgotten how to dream for herself. "I don't know, Marcus."

Marcus nodded, firing up his motorcycle. "Just as I thought." He roared down the highway.

⁂

Lily gave the sheriff's department two weeks' notice to find a replacement.

Todd went to school that Tuesday after Labor Day. The sooner he faced his friends, the teachers, and the questions, the better. His mother agreed to get him into counseling. The D.A. was arranging for him to do community service because of the stolen car and for battering an officer.

Lily dove into the meth lab case paperwork. Already she'd been notified that the two teens had coughed up the names of six adults in the ring. One of them knew her brother, but refused to say where he was, which angered Lily. That also helped convince her that her decision to leave this all behind was the right one, no matter what Marcus said. She'd come here because of her brother; she had to leave to try and find him. She'd talk to everybody she could from his most recent rehab center; she'd find some clue to his whereabouts.

Lily made the Superior daily paper's front page. She made the front page again on Wednesday and did three television interviews. She wasn't a dummy. She knew that her strawberry-blonde looks and uniform made for good visuals.

She was cleaning out a desk drawer in her office when Tootsie walked in with Lulu on one arm and a gift box in the other. Lily cringed, but plastered on a smile. Tootsie wore lavender capris with a top to match her fuzzy chicken.

"You're too late, Tootsie," Lily said. "The guy from the television station just left."

"I stopped him on the street outside. Lulu's gonna be on the six o'clock news."

"Oh."

"But that's not why I'm here. Our beaver man is packing up."

Lily's heartbeat tripped. She assumed he left yesterday. "Seems we're all packing up."

"That's just it. You have to stop him."

"That's not my job."

"Get over yourself. You're still in uniform. Arrest the man. Do something."

"Why is he so important to you?"

Lulu pecked at the buttons straining to contain Tootsie's bosom. Tootsie petted the chicken. "My silkies. Whenever he leaves the pen to go back to his RV, they try to get out of the pen to follow him. One day, Priscilla did. She almost got run over by a truck. Do you know how valuable my chickens are?"

Lulu clucked to punctuate the point.

"I can't help you, Tootsie."

"You're going to have to because the silkies are so agitated that I'm not sure Lulu's clutch will be hatching."

"Surely you're not accusing me of--"

"Yes. Chick murder."

To Lily's shock, Tootsie set Lulu and the gift box in front of Lily and raced out. Lily hurried to the door, "Tootsie? Get back here."

Tootsie called over her shoulder, "Last I saw him he was heading down the highway in that godawful rolling house of his."

"I'm not chasing after him for you."

"You're just too much of a big pile of chicken shit, you know that?"

Lily blinked hard, not sure she'd heard right. She recalled Kirsten telling her that Tootsie would get around to telling her she was "too" something. But chicken poop?

Tootsie called out as she got into her car, "By the way, the mayor and the chamber of commerce took a vote. You did a good job. We want you to stay as deputy."

"But you just said--"

"You're too chicken. Yes, that's what I said."

Too chicken? Lily stared at the lavender hen pecking about the papers on her desk. Now what? She had to finish packing. She backed off from the hen. Lulu clucked at her, the beady eyes almost mournful.

The odd freeing feeling--reminiscent of the feeling she had when Marcus told her "Wow" and she impulsively gave him the gritty kiss--came back. With a gingerly touch, she picked up Lulu. The cottony hen settled into her arms.

Lily noticed something odd about the gift box. It didn't smack of Tootsie. The box, about the size of a laptop, was wrapped in tasteful white tissue paper with a yellow ribbon and bow.

After putting Lulu down next to it, Lily opened the box. It was a clarinet.

Her heart burst. The clarinet's silver-toned keys sparkled. The black ebony had been polished to a high gloss. She found a note. *"This is what I mean about your hopes and dreams. Learn to play your clarinet. Do it just for you. Join an orchestra. Join a band and march to your own drummer. Look forward, not back. Your friend, Marcus."*

She and Lulu found the RV at a rest stop along Highway 53. Marcus, in a clean, white t-shirt and tan shorts, was inspecting the fasteners holding his motorcycle onto a trailer behind the RV. Lily's heart pounded against her chest wall. Lulu pecked at her badge.

"You're under arrest," she told him, walking over with Lulu in her arms.

He smiled. "Now that's a dangerous weapon."

She handed over Lulu. "She's been mourning you. Tootsie says you can't leave. The eggs may not hatch if you leave."

"But I have to. Classes and all that. I'm already late."

Now what? Why was she so miserable at this? Because her parents had always talked for her, that was why. It was time she ponied up her own gumption. Hadn't Marcus said she was "wow" and "intense"?

She said, "It's beautiful."

The sun highlighted his prominent cheekbones. "The clarinet."

"No, the message." She choked.

"Can't cry?"

She shook her head. "Not when in uniform."

Marcus looked about, then came up to her, petting Lulu. "Maybe you should get out of uniform."

She gulped. She couldn't even think. She stared at the ridiculous chicken.

"Gotta have dreams," he said. "Gotta take a chance. Gotta play your own music."

He gave her a kiss that made her hear clarinet notes on the breeze, made her smell his earthiness and the autumn goldenrod in bloom.

When he backed away, Lulu, still in his arms, was shaking her fuzzy head. The chicken made Lily smile. "You embarrassed her with the kiss, I think."

"She's jealous."

"About time it was the other way around. You and those chickens were starting to worry me."

The breeze kicked up again. Marcus looked up at the sky, sobering. "I gotta go, Lily. Long drive ahead of me."

When he handed Lulu back, Lily panicked. *Quadruple crap.* She couldn't let him leave. Not after a kiss that made her body play in harmony like a thousand instruments.

"Marcus, I've changed my mind. I'm staying in Moonstone. I'm keeping my job."

He ran a hand through his unruly hair. "Why? It's sort of crazy around here."

She hefted Lulu. "I want to hear my mother's reaction when I tell her about the lavender chicken. I'd like to tell her all about the giant beaver. What about you? You got some more beavers to dig up around Moonstone? Any possible reason to come back?"

Her heart swelled toward foolish hope.

He eyed her with suspicion. "Lily, do you really need me? I mean, you're so together, everything in its place, neat, in control, and I'm a mess. I'm even late for my classes."

She smiled, raising one hand to show him what was she'd done. "Cut all my nails off. I ripped a couple off out there in the woods, got dirt under the rest. And I felt the best about myself in a long time. You acted proud of me, too, which meant everything to me. You said 'Wow'. I need you, Marcus. But do you need me?"

Forget hummingbirds. Her heart was thundering on "idle" worse than his motorcycle.

He put Lulu in Lily's car, then he leaned against the door, his arms folded. "Yeah, I got a need. I...need to do a lot more research for all those books I'm going to write for our children."

"Our children?" The orchestra in her heart was tuning up. "Marcus, I was about to make the biggest, most bone-headed mistake of my life. When you said love was blind, you meant me, didn't you?"

"I was head over heels in love with you from the first time you came to see me and you stepped in chicken crap."

She laughed, appreciating what Tootsie had said--that she was too chicken for this man. "Does it matter to you that Kirsten and Tootsie may have been matchmaking?"

"I heard matchmaking runs rampant in Moonstone. Probably needs a woman with a badge to keep it in check."

She gave him a beguiling look and began unbuttoning her shirt. "Later. I'm off-duty."

He picked her up, swinging her around, the birch trees and birds and clouds gliding by in kaleidoscope, merging with the music playing in her heart.

"I love you, Marcus. I need you."

Moments later, inside his RV, he took his time showing her how much he loved and needed her. On his very, very happy sheets.

Much later, she finally noticed something. "Marcus, you ironed the sheets?"

"Not only that, I washed them!"

"How romantic. I love you."

"I love you. Were you really jealous of the chickens?"

"Oh yeah, you oaf. Now come here."

Lulu hatched her clutch of eight chicks that September. Two precious lavender-hued youngsters were among the brood. Tootsie gave one to Lily.

Henri and Felicity decided they wanted to continue dating that autumn. Ruth went on a safari in Africa.

Marcus applied for a teaching job at the nearby Superior campus of the University of Wisconsin; his new job would start in January.

A cute photo of the "hat" in the woman deputy's arms made it to newspapers around the world, even to Santiago, Chile, where Jason Schuster tucked it away under his cowboy hat for future reference.

85

If you enjoyed this author's book, then please place a review up at the site of purchase, and any social media sites you frequent!

You can find ALL our books up on our website at:

http://www.writers-exchange.com

All our romances:

http://www.writers-exchange.com/category/genres/romance/

All Christine's Books:

http://www.writers-exchange.com/christine-desmet/

About the Author

Christine **DeSmet** is an award-winning fiction writer and professional screenwriter. She is the author of the bestselling *Fudge Shop Mystery Series* and the popular novella series called *Mischief in Moonstone*.

She is a Distinguished Faculty Associate in Writing at University of Wisconsin-Madison where she teaches novel writing and screenwriting and directs the annual summer Write-by-the-Lake Writer's Workshop & Retreat. Through her master classes she has seen many of her adult students become published.

She is also a professional writing coach in the UW-Madison Writers' Institute conference's Pathway to Publication program.

Christine is a member of Mystery Writers of America, Sisters in Crime, Wisconsin Writers Association, Wisconsin Screenwriters Association, and other professional associations.

Christine is active on Facebook and you can also find her at http://www.ChristineDeSmet.com

Christine's author page at Writers Exchange E-Publishing is: http://www.writers-exchange.com/christine-desmet/

If you want to read more about books by this author, they are listed on the following pages...

Fudge Shop Mystery Series

Deadly Fudge Divas

A taste of trouble is in the air when a group of well-heeled, fudge-loving women descend on Ava Oosterling's newly acquired and lovingly refurbished bed & breakfast inn for a chocolate lovers' getaway.

When one of the women turns up dead--and Ava's grandfather is a prime suspect--Ava plunges into the thick of a murder case stickier than her candy store's line of Fairy Tale fudge flavors and the chocolate facials the women adore at the local spa.

It's springtime and the start of the tourist season in Fishers' Harbor, Wisconsin. Ava has opened the Blue Heron Inn with the help of handsome construction worker Dillon Rivers. Unfortunately, Dillon's mother--Ava's ex-mother-in-law--is among the secretive divas who become suspects along with Grandpa.

Ava turns for help from her friends but they have troubles, too. One is eager for a wedding proposal to unfold on live television, while another friend is expecting her first baby and asks Ava to assist with the birth.

Everything and everybody Ava loves seems in chaos--her fudge shop, her inn, her family, and her own friendships... Until she uncovers a thirty-year-old secret of the "deadly fudge divas".

Publisher: https://www.writers-exchange.com/deadly-fudge-divas/

Undercover Fudge

Candy shop owner Ava Oosterling has her hands full when her best friend Pauline Mertens takes a summer job as a wedding coordinator--with the nuptials and reception scheduled in mere days in the back yard of Ava's Blue Heron Inn overlooking Lake Michigan's bay.

To help out her best friend, Ava is intent on making the table favors-- edible fudge lighthouses patterned after their county's 11 lighthouses.

Unfortunately, trying to finish the luscious ruby chocolate lighthouses becomes elusive. The sheriff informs Ava that a band of thieves storming the country may have targeted this wedding. And that's because there's proof Pauline's mother is associated with the thieves.

When the sheriff asks Ava to go undercover, she finds herself in an emotional quagmire. Pauline's mother only recently returned to Fishers' Harbor after years of estrangement from her daughter. And, Coletta Mertens now works as the housekeeper at Ava's inn. Has Ava's fudge-and-wine hospitality provided a hideout for a criminal?

Unfortunately, "until death do us part" takes a murderous twist involving Ava's Grandpa Gil, the dog Lucky Harbor, and Ava's own beau.

Publisher: https://www.writers-exchange.com/undercover-fudge/

Holly Jolly Fudge Folly

An early, deep snow has gifted Fishers' Harbor, Wisconsin, with a perfect setting for the holiday celebration. Unfortunately removing snow from Main Street for the parade reveals the dead tax assessor with a knife in him-- containing Grandpa Gil's fingerprints.

It's clearly a setup and one that keeps Ava and Grandpa Gil under the watchful eyes of Sheriff Tollefson. Who wants Grandpa to miss playing Santa Claus in the Christmas parade and why? Who's being naughty instead of nice?

Grandpa doesn't help his case with talk of leaving town for good--words that chill Ava worse than the weather. She can't imagine life without Grandpa's warm hugs and laughter.

When vandals strike the historic shop and someone leaves Ava and fiancé Dillon Rivers for dead in the snow, Ava wonders if she may need the magical help of Santa's elves to solve the holiday folly.

Publisher: https://www.writers-exchange.com/holly-jolly-fudge-folly/

Mischief in Moonstone Series

Nestled against the sparkling shores of Lake Superior, the tiny village of Moonstone is anything but ordinary. Between romantic entanglements, quirky neighbors, and mysteries that seem to pop up with every season, the locals know life here comes with a generous dose of laughter and surprise. From silkie chickens and a giant prehistoric beaver skeleton to kidnapped reindeer and holiday hijinks, mischief is always waiting just around the corner. Fall in love with the humorous, heartwarming adventures of Moonstone--where romance meets mayhem in the most delightful ways.

Novella 1: When Rudolf was Kidnapped

Crystal Hagan's first-graders are in panic mode. Their beloved holiday reindeer, Rudolph, has been stolen from the school's live Christmas display. Without him, the children are convinced Christmas is canceled.

The trail of mischief leads to Peter LeBarron, the wealthy recluse who lives in a mansion locals call the "North Pole." To Crystal's shock, Peter freely admits to taking Rudolph--but he refuses to give him back without some romantic negotiations of his own.

With the holiday countdown ticking, Crystal must juggle her students' worries, a stolen reindeer, and an unexpected suitor who may have just stolen her heart.

Humorous, heartwarming, and filled with small-town Christmas magic, this novella is perfect for fans of cozy romance and holiday cheer.

Publisher: https://www.writers-exchange.com/when-rudolph-was-kidnapped/

Novella 2: Misbehavin' in Moonstone

Kirsten Peplinski has worked hard to open her dream restaurant on the shores of Lake Superior. But when the men of Moonstone start disappearing in the evenings--and her business suffers--she discovers the shocking reason: a touring boat offering topless entertainment just outside town limits.

Determined to put an end to the mischief, Kirsten confronts the boat's infuriatingly handsome owner, Jonathon VanBrocklin. Instead of backing down, Jonathon kidnaps her--claiming undressing and marriage are the only items on his menu.

Caught between outrage and unexpected attraction, Kirsten faces the wildest adventure of her life. Will she escape this reckless scheme, or discover that true love sometimes arrives in the most mischievous packages?

Humorous, romantic, and funny, cheeky, and charming, *Misbehavin' in Moonstone* is a sizzling small-town escape.

Publisher: https://www.writers-exchange.com/misbehavin-in-moonstone/

Novella 3: Mrs. Claus and the Moonstone Murder

New county deputy Lily Schuster is still learning the ropes when trouble strikes in Moonstone, Wisconsin. On her second day, she arrests archaeologist Marcus Linden for trespassing--only to find herself turning to him for help when a pie contest judge ends up murdered.

The suspects? None other than Henri LeBarron, the town's beloved eighty-four-year-old Santa, and his scandalous new companion, the alluring Felicity Starr. Both women are vying to become "Mrs. Claus" for the upcoming winter celebration--and their rivalry has turned deadly.

With August heat bearing down and tempers flaring, Lily must solve the case, keep her wits about her, and decide if Marcus's kisses are worth more than his alibis.

Quirky, romantic, and full of small-town mischief, *Mrs. Claus and the Moonstone Murder* blends mystery with a heart-stealing romance.

Publisher: https://www.writers-exchange.com/mrs-claus-and-the-moonstone-murder/

Novella 4: When the Dead People Brought a Dish-to-Pass

Three days before Halloween, Alyssa Swain finds a dead man in his car. But when she returns with help, the body has vanished.

Things only get stranger when the supposed corpse--scruffy, tall John Christopherson--appears on her doorstep very much alive...or at least claiming to be. John insists she summoned him to help prepare for a Halloween party, and he refuses to leave her house--or her heart.

But midnight on Halloween looms, and Alyssa must find a way to keep John from crossing into the afterlife forever.

Funny, eerie, and tender, When the Dead People Brought a Dish-to-Pass is a paranormal romance that blends small-town charm with Halloween magic.

Publisher: https://www.writers-exchange.com/when-the-dead-people-brought-a-dish-to-pass/

Novella 5: A Moonstone Wedding

Margie Mueller thought wedding jitters were normal--until her fiancé sent her a fertility rug.

She's no spring chicken, and the idea of raising a brood of Farina babies makes her panic. But before she can call the whole thing off, Tony's boisterous family descends on Moonstone with their parties, opinions, and endless interference.

Then a dead man turns up--wrapped in that same fertility rug. Suddenly, Margie's wedding isn't just in danger of collapsing under family chaos--it's at the center of a murder mystery. And Tony may know more than he's admitting.

Funny, quirky, and laced with small-town mischief, A Moonstone Wedding is a romantic novella with a deadly twist.

Publisher: https://www.writers-exchange.com/a-moonstone-wedding/

Novella 6: The Moonstone Fire

John "Bozeman" Hall has seen it all--longhorn cattle, grizzly hunts, even rattlesnake suppers. But nothing prepares him for Moonstone, Wisconsin.

When a suspicious fire destroys the newlyweds Crystal and Peter LeBarron's farm cabin, Bozeman is determined to track down the arsonist. His first suspect? A young homeless mother and her son, squatting in a cave on the property.

But the closer he gets to the truth, the more Bozeman discovers that danger isn't the only spark in town--so is the pull of unexpected love.

The Moonstone Fire delivers a sizzling blend of small-town mystery, heartwarming romance, and the quirky mischief Moonstone is known for.

Publisher: https://www.writers-exchange.com/the-moonstone-fire/

Coming November 2025...

Novella 7: All She Wore Was a Bow

Kincaid Hunter, professional bull rider and decorated veteran, has never been tamed--least of all by the thought of marriage. But when a good friend back home in Wisconsin plans a Christmas wedding, Kincaid can't resist riding in to try and stop him from making what he thinks is a big mistake.

What Kincaid doesn't expect is to be lassoed himself--by a wedding planner dressed as Mrs. Claus, with a sparkle in her eyes and a bow for every occasion.

Soon, the cowboy who vowed he'd never walk down the aisle discovers that love can tie a knot tighter than any rope.

All She Wore Was a Bow is a festive small-town romance full of humor, heart, and holiday magic.

Publisher: https://www.writers-exchange.com/the-moonstone-fire/

Coming Soon:

Novella 8: Pest Control

Novella 9: The Big Love & Murder Shilly-Shally in Moonstone

You can find ALL our books up on our website at:

http://www.writers-exchange.com

All our romances:

http://www.writers-exchange.com/category/genres/romance/

All Christine's Books:

http://www.writers-exchange.com/christine-desmet/

www.ingramcontent.com/pod-product-compliance
Lightning Source LLC
Chambersburg PA
CBHW052141150726
48002CB00003B/1016